*A*my looks up at Misty. "Excuse us, but Portia and I are focusing on serious business here."

Misty insists, "This is about a missing grasshopper with only three legs. I'd say that's pretty serious." She sighs. "How will she ever survive without me?"

Amy just shakes her head in an "I told you so" sort of way, slipping her fashion sketch into the center of her pop-star-emblazoned homework folder. "Portia, text me when you're ready to get serious about beautification."

Caught in the middle, all I can do is just nod okay. In an attempt to escape this tense girl triangle, I take out my PDA to make a few quick notes.

OBSERVATION: Amy and Misty appear to be from different planets, both of which are currently circling the same galaxy, and unless I figure out a solution soon, they are about to collide!

Hays, Anna.
Portia's exclusive and
confidential rules on tr
2009.
33305218522849
gi   01/07/10

Portia's Exclusive and Confidential Rules on True Friendship

ANNA HAYS

miX

ALADDIN MIX
NEW YORK   LONDON   TORONTO   SYDNEY

If you purchased this book without a cover, you should be aware that this book is stolen property. It was reported as "unsold and destroyed" to the publisher, and neither the author nor the publisher has received any payment for this "stripped book."

This book is a work of fiction. Any references to historical events, real people, or real locales are used fictitiously. Other names, characters, places, and incidents are the product of the author's imagination, and any resemblance to actual events or locales or persons, living or dead, is entirely coincidental.

ALADDIN MIX

Simon & Schuster Children's Publishing Division

1230 Avenue of the Americas, New York, NY 10020

Text copyright © 2009 by Anna Hays

All rights reserved, including the right of reproduction
in whole or in part in any form.

ALADDIN PAPERBACKS and related logo and ALADDIN MIX
and related logo are registered trademarks of Simon & Schuster, Inc.

Designed by Karin Paprocki

The text of this book was set in Cochin.

Manufactured in the United States of America

First Aladdin MIX edition May 2009

2 4 6 8 10 9 7 5 3 1

Library of Congress Control Number 2009920708

ISBN: 978-1-4169-7806-0

For Buzz,
my true friend

ACKNOWLEDGMENTS

Friendship is everything. For Clare, Carol, Roxanne, Chesley, Mary, Amy, and all of my friends who are the magic formula for my joy and happiness.

Special thanks to . . .

Liesa for her gentle touch, Dan for his unwavering support, and Matt for believing in Portia and me from the very beginning.

Elsa and Norman, you wrote the book on true friendship.

Mom, Susie, Stevie, Hannah, Joey, Olivia, Mary, Sophie, Josie, Elaine, Larry, and my whole family, whose love and devotion inspire me everyday.

And to the coolest and most loyal friends I could ever ask for, Benjamin and Will.

Portia's
Exclusive and Confidential
Rules on True Friendship

Chapter 1

Loretta was hungry. She looked into the refrigerator, but all she saw were three jars of apricot jam and an old bottle of ketchup. She then checked the candy jar, but came up empty there, too. Nothing but a sticky old cherry lollipop. Suddenly she remembered that she had hidden exactly $3.66 under her pillow. She raced to see if it was still there, and it was! Now she could buy something to eat. If a stick of grape swirl licorice cost twelve cents, then how many sticks of licorice could Loretta buy with her hidden stash?

Math! What an incredibly irrelevant subject. Aren't there other bigger problems in the world to solve than a strange girl's candy budget? There is world hunger, overpopulation, and I'm pretty sure there are hundreds of animals going extinct every day. And Miss Killjoy is having us ponder a totally ridiculous and fictional shopping spree? I'm not even allowed to let candy enter my household. It's a major Indigo (she's my mom) violation to even think about refined sugar. So this whole math exercise relates to my life as much as hot chocolate marshmallow fudge does to agave-sweetened soy carob pudding!

Since Indigo is a health food chef and restaurant owner of a local organic eatery called Contentment (aka The Tent), my house, and in particular my refrigerator, is a no-sugar zone. Instead it's packed with fresh vegetables and fruits handpicked from our overgrown backyard garden. In our sputtery ancient refrigerator, you can also find recyclable containers of every possible size, filled with food experiments created by Indigo herself for The Tent's ever-morphing menu. Many of these food combinations will most likely never make it past our driveway, but to my "good fortune," they do make it to our dining room table almost every meal.

I try to focus on what Miss Killjoy is teaching us, but the numbers and decimal points blur together until my eyes cross. I switch pencils, adjust the angle of my head, tuck my hair behind my ears for better listening, but still I find it hard to pay attention. It sounds like she's repeating the same words over and over again.

IMPORTANT FACT: Miss K. is threatening a pop math quiz any day, so there's extra pressure to stay alert.

THREE POSSIBLE REASONS FOR MY CURRENT GRUMPY STATE:

1. Winter break has been over for approximately seven hours. Now there will be no more homework-free days until spring!
2. Miss Killjoy will not be getting an award for "entertainer of the year" any time soon.
3. Nothing is ever new at Palmville Middle School. It's just one extra large homework-spitting factory that's been stealing kids' free time for about a zillion years!

NOTE: If anyone reads this, please gently remind Miss Killjoy and her other teacher "friends" that life is more than juggling compound numbers. And that, in my not-so-humble opinion, acute angles are not even remotely cute. Big thanks! Signed, Portia Avatar.

As I look out the large floor-to-ceiling window of our classroom, I see the quiet semitropical small town of Palmville, California, just beyond the tall palm trees that border the middle school's parking lot. I imagine that right now Indigo is in the back office of The Tent, figuring out how many pomegranates she'll be ordering today for a new round of menu-tasting. There's more than a 70 percent chance that her mind is swimming with thoughts of organic ingredients for just the right food combination that she will serve to her loyal customers, who expect only the healthiest and the most delectable creations from her. My taste buds, on the other hand, don't always agree with Indigo's 100 percent organic and cruelty-free food experiments. My idea of a fortified breakfast consists of an oversize bowl of Frosted Flakes with two lightly toasted strawberry Pop-Tarts for dessert.

Just around the corner from Indigo's office, past the storage cabinet and walk-in refrigerator, you will find The Tent's assistant chef, Hap Lester, who is just shy of thirty years old. He is chopping away at an assortment of sweet onions for the late breakfast rush, perfecting a Spanish omelet with a new twist. He barely misses his index finger midway through one of his expert chops. That's because he's caught in a daydream starring none other than my mother, whom he imagines will recognize his true love for her one day and then fall deeply and hopelessly in love with him.

Suddenly Miss Killjoy's high-pitched voice sends me soaring back to middle school reality. With an "I just wolfed a whole bowl of super sour lemons" puckery smile, she asks, "Portia, what do you think the solution is?"

Oh no! My temporary mind vacation has led to a potentially disastrous result and a further rift in the not-so-compatible ongoing relationship between me and mathematics. I open my mouth, hoping that my brain will provide me with just the right word combination to rescue me from this math jam. Just then, by some miracle of awesome timing in the universe, someone knocks on the classroom door. In walks a shy-looking girl, clutching a shiny purple retainer case like it's the last one on the planet Earth.

Miss K. welcomes the new girl. "Class, this is Misty Longfellow. She just arrived from Precipitation, Oregon. I want you all to give Misty a great big sunny Palmville welcome."

Halfheartedly and terribly out of sync, the whole class attempts a communal greeting. "Welcome, Misty."

Misty lifts her head slightly and manages a quarter of a wave. She responds with a quivering whisper. "Thank you."

Miss K. then leads her to the empty seat just to the right of me. Misty's head faces in the downward direction of the classroom floor the entire time she makes her way to her seat. Just as she's about to sit down, she drops her retainer case and shrieks at the top of her lungs, "My Ralphie!"

I'm not sure, but I think I see a furry black thing with eight legs that looks suspiciously like a spider crawl past my olive flats. Hold on, it is a spider!

For the first time in the history of seventh grade, I see

Miss K.'s sour-lemon smile fade away. She screams, "It's a spider! Okay, nobody panic. It's only a SPIDER!"

Twenty-two kids plus one terrified teacher equals total chaos. The only three kids who aren't freaking out about the runaway spider are Misty, Webster (the class brain with the sparkling green eyes), and me. Remembering what Indigo has always taught me about being kind to all living things, I zero in on Ralphie. He's crawling stealthily up Miss Killjoy's chair, about to nose-dive into her leather briefcase. I take out a lavender-tinted tissue from my convenient pocket pack and silently make a beeline for the confused spider. I corner him, take a long deep breath, and then scoop him up with the tissue.

Meanwhile, Misty zigzags between the disordered desks that used to be set in neat rows before Ralphie decided to make an escape. She opens her retainer case, excitedly insisting that I place Ralphie inside, which I do, tissue and all. Snap. The case closes, and Ralphie is back home safely.

Misty then leaps over a chair, catching my left elbow as I return to my desk. "You did it! You are Ralphie's savior. You must surely have a name."

I take two steps back and answer her. "Portia."

Misty freezes. With her eyes glazed over, she utters, "That's a magnificent name. Do you have a last one too?"

"Avatar."

"Portia Avatar! That is the most perfect name I truly have ever heard in my entire life. It is unbelievably amazing to meet you, Portia Avatar." She giggles as the rest of the class, including Miss Killjoy, slowly straighten themselves out and slide their desks back to their pre-Ralphian positions, pretending that the last five minutes of their lives never actually happened.

Then the bell rings. Miss Killjoy is so concerned about making a speedy exit from the classroom that she forgets to give us tomorrow's homework assignment.

NOTE: I never knew that a creepy-looking black spider could be such a good luck charm!

Chapter 2

*A*my is midway through one of her famous Clamdigger monologues. "P., I am so excited for *moi.* Yesterday Mama agreed that I deserved another sparkling new pair of wedged flip-flops and so, yes, they are ordered, purchased, and waiting for me as we speak. I got the confirmation e-mail this morning."

"That's so cool, Ame. I'm incredibly thrilled for you." I look down at my worn pair of flats and plot how I will convince Indigo that I deserve a sparkling new pair in a different color next time. Maybe blossoming pink. I quietly determine that my wardrobe is in need of a serious rescue mission if it's going to survive the rest of the school year.

Amy continues, "Life is delectable. I can't think of anyone else I'd rather be right now. Maybe the Queen of England. Erase that thought. She's ancient. I guess that leaves little young me again."

Sometimes I have to tune out Amy's random meanderings. I know that she basically means well, but she has this weird habit of thinking too much about herself. She gets so caught up in Amy with a capital A that she forgets about her best friends, for example, Portia with a capital P.

FACT: Amy Clamdigger has been my best friend since kindergarten. We share almost everything—our top secrets and even our confidential crushes. If I were to make a list of my top ten friends of all time so far in my twelve years on Earth, the Amester would be at the top. Even though she gets stuck in Amy's world a lot, she is always there for me when I truly need her.

As I think about Amy and look around at the other tables with groups of kids huddled together at the same spots they have claimed since the first day of school, I wonder what makes a friend a friend.

QUESTION: What are the ingredients of a true friend?

I slide my PDA from the side pocket of my knapsack and type in the following: "Portia's Exclusive and Confidential Rules on True Friendship." Careful not to attract attention, I pretend that I'm checking my horoscope, while I clandestinely type in my first rule.

FRIENDSHIP RULE #1: True friends stick by you, no matter what!

Then I look up from my PDA to experience a strange moment. Silence. Amy Clamdigger silent? She stares me down with suspicious eyes. I fumble, then regain my composure. I search for a way to fill the dead air space with a fictional account to distract Amy. Scrambling, I say, "Cozmik Newz reports that my intuitive powers will be on overdrive today!"

"So what else is new? Your brain is always on the

lookout for something unusual." She takes a bite of her grilled-cheese-and-tomato pressed sandwich, then surprises me. She asks me something about myself. "How's the case going with your missing-but-somewhere-in-the-universe father? Is he still halfway across the globe?"

"Not sure yet. Being a Girl Psychoanalytic Detective definitely has its ups and downs."

"So what's it today? Up or down?"

"I'd have to say it's moving in a downward direction at the moment."

IMPORTANT NOTE: I should mention that I am a Girl Psychoanalytic Detective, and I solve the mysteries of people. I strongly believe that people have many sides worth investigating, with hidden truths that for some reason or another are not brought to the surface. That's where I step in. My first case stars Patch, my missing father, whom I have never met. After the big earthquake a few months ago, I discovered a photograph of him. Indigo, who until a few months ago had refused to disclose even .75 of an ounce of a clue about him, has now agreed to help me with my search to find him. But progress remains slow.

Suddenly, from the shadows of the endless rows of plastic cafeteria chairs, Misty appears, leaning over my shoulder. "You're the one!"

I decide to interpret her mysterious comment as a compliment and thank her. She just stands there with her feet glued to the ground; not even her toes move. Then she sits down in an available plastic chair at our table. She nervously tries to join in on my conversation with Amy. She begins with a question. "Did you say 'detective'?"

QUESTIONS: Has Misty been listening to me and Amy C.? How long has she been standing behind us?

As I try to figure out if I'm going to reveal my double identity as a detective to "new girl," I watch Misty adjust her wire-framed glasses, which are hopelessly bent out of shape. She can't wait another second for my response. "Did I do something wrong? It's just that I think you're incredible, Portia Avatar. You're utterly and completely the person I've been looking for since preschool."

Amy, meanwhile, pores over her new copy of Kewl Teenz magazine, refusing to even acknowledge Misty's presence at the table. Every once in a while, I hear a loud, exaggerated sigh emerging from Amy's side of the table from behind the fluorescent glossy teen zine. For a split second, Amy even turns her head to check out the exchange between me and Misty. That's when I hear a loud scream. Amy leaps dramatically from her chair, sending it flying across the cafeteria, bouncing like an oversize toddler's toy. She points madly in the direction of the table, shrieking, "That thing is back!"

Then I see it too. Misty has brought Ralphie back for his second school visit of the day. She stumbles out of her chair and starts chasing Amy around the cafeteria, opening and closing the purple retainer case, insisting that Ralphie has been safely relocated, promising that the only thing that resides in her retainer case now is her red-tinted plastic molded retainer. Amy screams anyway, "Get that thing away from me!"

The rest of the kids in the near vicinity crack up at the live comedy act that's totally free of charge. Before you can say "super-awkward moment," Amy has vanished out the door, clinging to her designer tote, which contains half of her life. Her more-than-a-little-bit perfect hair is less than perfect now, which is by my calculation what's really upsetting her most.

I slowly walk toward the overturned chair and make believe that no one is watching me as I drag it back to the table. When I sit down again, I check my lemon yellow daisy wristwatch, wishing and hoping that time will pass faster than usual, even though it's against the laws of astronomy. There's exactly four minutes and thirty seconds left until the bell rings.

Misty stares into my eyes and declares, "I have a case for you to solve. It's about a very close friend of mine who is in desperate trouble."

I don't even blink. "Sorry, Misty. I've got a major case on my hands that still needs solving."

Wearing every emotion on her face, including sad, worried, excited, and anxious, Misty plows ahead. "It's only someone's life at stake!"

After a long pause followed by an ocean of anticipation, I ask her, "Are you serious?"

 15

Then the bell rings.

Misty completely ignores it. "Yes! Detective Avatar, would you leave a friend out in the cold? I know you better than that."

QUESTION: Has Misty checked the weather lately?

IMPORTANT NOTE: Since the wildfires have decided to make their unwanted entrance to Palmville, the temperature is way hot, hovering around the high nineties. It's not cold in the least, not even with air-conditioning. And besides, Misty doesn't "know" Portia Avatar. I've spoken maybe twenty-five words to her. But I must admit, this new girl is certainly different. Maybe because of her unusualness, the case might be worth pursuing.

I find myself saying, "Let's talk more about your 'friend in need' later at my mom's restaurant, Contentment. I'll be there after four."

Misty skips in place. "You mean you might actually consider the case? This is the most joyful news I've heard all century!" She stops skipping. "I forgot to tell you one thing. No one must know anything about this. It's top secret."

I assure Misty that it's my job as a girl detective to keep secrets. I'm a professional.

She responds, "Absolutely, of course, for sure."

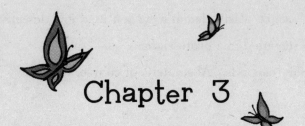

Chapter 3

3:03 P.M., HALLWAY,
PALMVILLE MIDDLE SCHOOL

I load up my books, preparing myself for a long afternoon of homework. As I place one five-pound book after another into my knapsack, I wonder about the case that new girl had brought up earlier at lunch.

QUESTIONS: What could it possibly be about? Who is the mysterious subject and what does she mean when she says a life is "at stake"? And why the big secret?

I grab one of the magenta shoulder straps of my book

bag and secure it under my arm, then feel around for the other strap, which is hanging just out of my reach. Suddenly Webster Holiday appears and hands me the strap. He gives me a half-moon smile. "Gravity can be so unkind, Miss Avatar."

FACT: Webster Holiday, age eleven (he skipped a grade), has the brightest green eyes in the entire five-mile radius of Palmville. He's also super smart and possesses a sly sense of humor. Sometimes his jokes fly over me like a soaring California bald eagle, but most of the time, I get what he's trying for, even if the punch line isn't always delivered with absolute grace and precision.

Adjusting the strap on my shoulder, I quietly say, "Thanks, Webster. Did you have even a vague idea of what Killjoy was talking about in class?" Forcing a laugh, I answered my own question. "Of course you did. You're a total math genius."

Webster's face remains 97 percent expressionless. "I've done the numbers and have determined that there's a high probability that Killjoy's math quiz will be sprung upon us in the next forty-two hours."

For some unknown reason, I get a major energy boost and continue on my word safari going nowhere. "I'm so not ready for it. Thanks for the warning, though. I know Miss K. is going to throw in some trick questions, and she always adds ridiculous bonus questions too."

I look around and notice there's no Webster anywhere anymore. It's just me talking to myself—with a surprise new guest. Miss Killjoy is standing right next to me. "Portia, is there something you want to discuss with me?"

Embarrassment central! "No, Miss Killjoy. I'm perfectly fine. Webster was here, and . . . never mind." Staring at my math textbook sitting on the top shelf of my locker, I decide to distract her from thinking too much about my peculiar behavior. "Wow, math is such a mind-boggling subject."

Miss K. smiles and responds, "I like to think so. Good afternoon, Portia!"

Before she picks up on the fact that my sincerity meter is way down below zero, I break free of her piercing eyes and make a run for it, out the door, down the hill covered with painted desert flowers, past the straight line of tall, skinny palms, through a man-made stone path toward town. I head to my after-school job helping out at the dusty wonderland Trash and Treasures, Palmville's one and only junk shop.

My brisk walk to Trash and Treasures is accompanied by a sweet-sounding medley of Palmville's finest bird residents. It's true that all the birds are extremely happy here. They sing about this fact day and night. My guess is that this widely varied bird population, which includes wild parrots, mockingbirds, catbirds, and nightingales, enjoys living in Palmville because the weather is nearly perfect, except of course for major earthquakes, severe droughts, flash floods, and seasonal wildfires. Whenever we're not experiencing a total natural disaster, life is pretty much blue skies and warm breezes.

FACT: Palmville was hit by a five-alarm earthquake back in the fall. After overtime days and nights of hammering, sawing, measuring, and building, The Tent (and the rest of the town) is up and operating again, which makes my mom, and therefore me, very content. The dust has settled around town and the rebuilding is well underway, and in some situations, even complete. But there are still obvious signs of post-earthquake damage around town, like the overabundance of cracks in the sidewalks on Main Street and the slanted steps leading up to the front door of Hansel's Hardware. But the only thing the weathermen (and women) report on these days are the crazy wildfires that lurk just outside town in the nearby canyons. It's fire season, and it's decided to arrive early this year.

I rub my eyes as I walk toward Main Street. The dryness in the air is a possible clue that maybe the wildfires are getting closer than the weatherpeople report on the news. I immediately erase that thought from my brain and instead weave through all the shortcuts I know by heart until I arrive just below the hand-painted sign that hangs at the entrance of Trash and Treasures.

3:24 P.M.,
TRASH AND TREASURES

It's always wisdom central with Trash and Treasures owner Vera Alloway. Her answers are usually questions. Her questions are almost always answers. And she makes you think in a way that doesn't feel like homework.

> **DESCRIPTION:** Vera has a definite personal style. Her year-round desert tan is accompanied by her salt-and-pepper short hair. The earrings she wears are created from broken pieces of gold and silver jewelry she handpicks herself from a treasure trove of long-forgotten heirlooms. Colorful clashing buttons are strung on a necklace created with two recycled chains skillfully clasped together. Her sandals are made of worn leather with long straps that tie around her ankles.

Announcement! If you have anything in your house that you think is worthless, broken, or out-of-date, give it to Vera. She'll make sure it's fixed and transformed into something amazing. Every day she carefully polishes, paints, and glues together combinations of collectibles, wobbly furniture, and formerly extraneous knickknacks. Vera strongly believes in second chances, especially for discarded pieces of junk.

Vera says she's old enough to know. I'm pretty sure

that means she's sixty-three. I have reason to believe that she reads minds, too. She can always tell what's on my mind before I even open my mouth. Even though Vera has been around since the last century, I've only gotten to know her over the past few months since the earthquake, when Indigo first volunteered my services at Trash and Treasures. At first it was, "Thanks, mom." But as I got to know Vera and her mystical secret world of junk, not to mention her endless supply of more-than-decent advice, it quickly became, "THANKS, MOM!"

I hear a muffled voice from Vera's mysterious back room. "Care for a pomegranate, Ms. Avatar?" The voice belongs to Vera. It grows louder as I see her walk toward me, clutching a dozen torn prom dresses. She places them in a messy pile next to me on the floor. "I never knew how heavy lace could be!" Then she hands me a pomegranate.

I happily accept the offering. "Indigo is going to love this. I'm sure she'll find a way to turn it into something 'interesting.' How did you know she was on a pomegranate mission?"

"I didn't."

Vera then directs me to the part of the store reserved

strictly for music. Faded sheet music balances on shelves, crooked concert posters line the wall, and prehistoric audiocassettes fill the secondhand wood-paneled bookcases. Vera invites me to help her sort through a new shipment of vinyl records.

> **NOTE:** A vinyl record is a plastic round saucer the size of an average steering wheel that has music programmed onto it. As it spins around on this contraption called a turntable, the music plays with this never-ending scratching sound on every tune. I can't believe people actually listened to songs this way and liked it! I totally feel sorry for them.

Vera selects one of the vinyl records. On the cover is a photo of a woman with big hair named Patsy Cline. The title of the album is Sentimentally Yours, and the word "Heartaches" also appears on the cover. Vera carefully slips it out and places it on the turntable. The music plays at full volume. Vera smiles a rare smile, then does a shuffle as she reaches for her trusty measuring tape. It's almost as if she's dancing. She looks at me with squinty eyes. "What happened to your necklace?"

I look down at the necklace I'm wearing today, a gift from Vera. The gold-plated shooting star hanging from a simple chain is now completely unrecognizable. "Ralphie did it! I swear I'm going to squish him the next time our paths cross!"

Vera looks at me with a sparkle in her eyes. "That's a pretty darn bold move, missy!"

"You don't understand. Ralphie has eight legs. Seven should serve him just fine!"

Vera crinkles her nose like she's got an itch.

I then recount the strange adventure of Misty and her deceptive retainer case. I describe Misty's cave-girl message to me about "being the one" and her out-of-the-blue-sky request for me to take on a new case featuring her alleged "friend in need." The more I tell Vera this unusual tale, the more she insists, "This Misty chickie sounds like a live one! Taking on this new case will only help sharpen your detective skills. As I see it, it's a no-lose situation, Ms. Avatar."

I look straight into Vera's eyes. I can't argue with her crystal-clear wisdom. I take a deep breath and then exhale. "Okay, I'll do it. But I think you should know that

I'm an incredibly busy person with miles of homework and a pop quiz on the way. I'm not sure there are enough hours, minutes, seconds, or even nanoseconds in the day or night to take on another case!"

Vera says with the cosmic patience of an old lioness, "You'll find a way."

She then disappears into the back office while I sort through recycled prom dresses to the scratchy country melody playing in the background. I decide to arrange the dresses by color instead of size, just to keep things entertaining. Almost an hour passes, and then the sound of a rooster's crow from my PDA signals that it's time to head off to Contentment. I lift the mechanical arm from the record player just at the point when Ms. Cline is singing about how she's longing for a lost love who had blue eyes. I turn off the record player and shout good-bye in the direction of Vera's office.

Vera responds, "So long, Portia. You know that you're on your way to a new discovery!"

I'm still not sure if taking on Misty's new mysterious case is the best timing. With some hesitation, I answer, "I hope so!"

Before I leave, Vera adds, "I'll see you next time. A new shipment of lamp shades is coming in on Wednesday. I'll need some help sorting them."

"I'm there!" And just like that, with my knapsack back on over my shoulders and a pomegranate in one hand, I'm out the door.

Under the Palmville sky, a handful of wild parrots flock from one tree to the next, chirping and flapping their way down the street, hovering just above me, like guardian angels, making sure I make the short trip to my mom's restaurant safely.

Chapter 4

A wooden flute plays softly over the hidden speakers. The Tent's renovation is nearly complete, except for a few touches. Hap wipes down the counter slowly and methodically, spacing out to the hypnotizing world fusion music over the speakers.

DESCRIPTION: After the earthquake, The Tent was restored to its original state, except for the kitchen area, which now consists of new and shiny stainless steel appliances. When it was first redone over a month ago, everything felt so clean, like that new car smell that is always impossible to recreate no matter how hard air freshener companies try to do it. But, just like new car smell, it's fleeting. So now, when I walk into The Tent, the scent of freshly ground curry has already seeped into the walls. And, today, just like every day starting at 8 a.m., organic free-trade coffee brews, filling the air with a rich coffee bean aroma that always reminds me of home, even though home is down the street and around the corner. Iced sun tea stews next to the open window near the front counter. Mismatched wooden tables purchased at neighboring flea markets are painted a rainbow of colors, inspired by the fruits and vegetables that grow in Indigo's two gardens, one outside the back of the restaurant, and the other in our very own backyard at home.

I'm just about to stir Hap from his zoned-out love-is-always-in-the-air state when Indigo enters from the back room, balancing a large hemp-woven basket filled with pomegranates. I notice that the pomegranates have a layer of dark dust on them.

I ask Indigo, "What's the latest news on the fires?"

Responding with her calm, lavender-blended-with-rosemary voice, "Rock dropped by The Tent a little while ago and says the fires are 40 percent contained."

 30

"Rock was visiting you? How does he come up with all this free time?"

Smiling, Indigo continues, "He's not that concerned, so you shouldn't be either, sweet Portia."

IMPORTANT FACT: Rock Neruda is a really muscular Palmville firefighter who has befriended my mother. He came snooping around just after the earthquake, and from what I gather, there is potential for a romance between them, but it seems to be just beyond their reach.

Indigo helps me take off my colossal knapsack, calling gently over to Hap, who is caught in a frozen stare with his eyes glued to her, "Why don't we give Portia a preview of the pomegranate smoothies we were exploring today?"

In a trembling voice, Hap manages, "Brilliant idea, Indigo."

My taste buds are not sure how brilliant the idea is yet, but I'm so hungry right now I could eat almost anything, including another one of Indigo's latest experiments with pomegranates.

My PDA then lights up, informing me that a new message has arrived. I check the sender, and it's none other than Amy the Clamdigger inquiring about my whereabouts.

To: pavatar@palmville.net
From: mememe@palmville.net

Excuse **moi** for asking, but I tried to find you after school and you were absolutely nowhere in sight. Fact or fiction: Were you with new girl? Just curious. BFF :) Amy

I'm about to respond to Amy's message when I notice an oddly shaped pendant swinging left to right in front of me. It belongs to Misty Longfellow. Her mouth sparkles from the purple-tinted full-on hardware wrapped around every tooth in her mouth. She looks around in awe. "Contentment is so utterly coolio! I cannot believe that you have the honor and privilege to come here whenever you want to and eat whatever you want to at this most specialicious paradise."

Hap notices my "new friend." He graciously brings over two freshly blended pomegranate smoothies, handing each of us one. Misty is overjoyed, and she breathlessly thanks Hap. "This is incredibly awesome!" She clutches the tall drink in her hands and takes a giant gulp of the magic pomegranate potion.

Moving slowly to an imaginary song, Misty barely holds on to her fruit drink while attempting a waltz. Slipping and sliding on the exposed wooden floor, she loses her balance, sending the pendant that was hanging around her neck across the dining tables to the other side of the room. She panics. "My Sweet Sunshine!" I watch as she carefully scoops up a mysterious miniature object, then places it inside her pendant. Her face looks 1,003 times more relaxed now. She sighs. "Welcome home, Sweet Sunshine!"

I try to get to the bottom of this strange behavior. "That necklace is interesting."

Misty responds, "Sweet Sunshine likes it too! So comfy cozy. Want to see?" She carefully opens the pendant, revealing a three-legged grasshopper. "Sweet Sunshine, meet Portia Avatar."

I manage a lame "Hello" to the grasshopper, while making a mental note of Misty's peculiar habit of carrying around small creeping and crawling insects.

Misty confesses, "Sunshine is just one of my many friends in need. I can't help myself. I see a grasshopper with three legs and I swear I hear her call out my name—'Save me, Misty!'—and before I know it, she's living in my latest fashion accessory."

While still figuring out why Misty is so rescue-crazy, I make an attempt to learn more about the new case. "So, this 'friend' of yours. What seems to be the trouble?"

"What friend?"

"Your friend. The one whose life is at stake?"

"Maxwell!"

Slowly I lean forward. "What seems to be Maxwell's problem?"

"It's something you have to see for yourself."

I put on my best detective face but say nothing.

IMPORTANT NOTE: Girl detectives must remember to wear their "detective" faces at all times, otherwise there's a chance they could jeopardize their various cases. That means no displaying any obvious signs of emotion, including super excitement, extreme fear, and/or total confusion.

Misty fills the silent void. "When you see Maxwell, you'll understand why this case is so important. He's waiting for you right now. Time is slipping away. We need you, P. Avatar."

Just then Indigo walks up to the table. She insists on meeting my "new friend." I politely introduce Misty to Indigo.

Misty leaps up and pleads with Indigo, "Please let your daughter come to my house now. We're going to study for a humongous surprise math quiz that could happen any time this week. I just moved here, and I absolutely need to get up to speed. And Portia is such a super amazing math student. She's the perfect person to help me!"

Indigo smiles and agrees to Misty's request, but only on the condition that I'm back home by six. Misty is so pleased that she pops out of her seat and starts dancing a waltz again.

FACT: For the next sixty minutes of my twelve-year-old life, I'll pretend to study for a random math quiz, when actually I'll be investigating a new subject whose name is Maxwell and whose life (according to the highly unusual new girl in town) appears to be absolutely and positively at stake.

Chapter 5

The wind picks up just as Misty and I head up the canyon road to her house. She's about five bike lengths ahead of me, but I'm miles away in my mind. I'm caught in a daydream that takes me across the town line, out to sea. I'm rowing a small weathered wooden boat with all my strength. Each time I row forward, the wind sends me back farther and farther to where I first started. Near the sandy shore now, I decide not to fight nature's powerful and forceful personality, so I drop the oars and let the wind pick a direction for me. Just before I decide how it's going to end, I hear my name being called out and snap out of the daydream.

It's Amy! What brings her to this part of town? She lives way over on the other side of Main Street. She shouts, "Did you get my warning?"

I stop my secondhand bike so quickly that the back tire skids left to right. "Amy, why are you here?"

She blurts out, "I was meeting a friend."

FACT: Amy Clamdigger does not have a friend who lives in the canyons.

QUESTION: Why is Amy acting so weird?

I ask her, "Is everything okay?" Then it occurs to me that I'm losing sight of Misty now. Before Amy can respond, I insist, "I've really got to go."

"I totally get it. It's all about new girl now, isn't it?"

"I'm on a case."

Amy raises her eyebrows as high as they will go. "Really?"

Misty finally notices that I'm not behind her and

turns around. She rides back toward me, calling out, "We're almost there, I promise!"

Amy starts to walk away, then turns and says, "If you're starting a new case, you're going to need a new wardrobe. Your current ensemble is all wrong for detective work." I look down at my panda bear pink tee and worn flare jeans. The self-proclaimed number one fashion diva of Palmville continues, "That's where moi fits in. Let me sleep on it and I'll get back to you with some ideas."

"Thanks, Ame. I have to get to work now."

Amy smiles. "You have gotten your tetanus shot, haven't you?"

By the time Misty arrives, Amy is yards away. She flips back her shoulder-length red hair and continues walking without looking back.

I jump back on my bike to finish the uphill ride. I'm seriously wondering if this case is worth the rocky mountain climb. I smell the spooky scent of smoke, and soon my eyes start to burn. I stop to rub them and then it happens. Webster H. appears from behind a monster jade tree to check the mailbox at the end of his long driveway. He looks as surprised as I am. He greets me, "Good afternoon, Ms. Avatar."

"Hello, Webster. I've really got to go." A pack of dogs in the distance starts barking.

"Of course you do, Portia. I've been meaning to ask you something." Then his words get drowned out by the out-of-tune dog chorus.

Misty speeds down the hill to retrieve me. "Hurry! Maxwell needs you!"

I turn to say good-bye to Webster. And in the handful of seconds we've been awkwardly standing together, I've planned out a mini-speech about how I'll see him in class tomorrow and how I'm seriously unprepared for the upcoming math quiz. But I don't get the chance to try out my new script, because W.H. is already back at his front door. Before I can count to five, the door has closed behind him and he's gone altogether.

QUESTIONS: I wonder what burning question Webster has to ask me. Could it possibly be a personal question such as, "Portia, are you busy on Friday for lunch?" or is it more the kind of question he usually asks me, like, "Excuse me, Portia, do you have the exact time?" or "Do you have any idea if it will be sunny next Thursday?"

FACT: Boys are certainly mysterious creatures. Especially this one.

5:17 P.M.,
MISTY'S BACKYARD

A tired-looking, dirty white bunny with black spots and droopy ears stares at me, looking severely depressed. This is Misty's "friend in need." I can't believe my eyes. I've seen bunnies before, but I've never traveled so far and biked up so high to actually meet one. Maxwell's makeshift home consists of a hand-me-down fleece blanket held up by a collection of crooked sticks. Before I take a closer look at my new subject, my PDA flashes. It's Amy with an urgent e-mail.

To: pavatar@palmville.net
From: mememe@palmville.net

Big news! I just discovered that I adore the intricate art of mathematics! It's so challenging, yet so blissfully logical. I can't get over what a natural I am at least common denominators. Such ridiculous joy to be able to speak math so fluently. How's your case going? World Peace! :) Amy

P.S. Have you ever considered stripes?

I ignore this message for now, and instead inspect my new subject more closely.

Misty emerges from a secret hiding place, carrying bits of potato peels in the palm of her hand. She sits on the ground next to me and proceeds to feed Sweet Sunshine, who's still residing in her pendant. "That's funny. I haven't heard a chirp from Sweet Sunshine since we left your mom's restaurant."

Then Misty downloads background data on how she found Maxwell. "We had just moved to Palmville, and I was exploring the backyard when I spotted poor Maxwell. He had dug himself a little secret spot in the far corner of the yard. I couldn't believe how sad he looked."

I stare into Maxwell's big, sorrowful eyes.

Misty continues with the case's backstory as I take notes on my trusty PDA. "My mom is one hundred percent fed up with my rescuing ways, and now that we've moved to Palmville, her no-pets-at-home policy is more strictly enforced than ever. If Maxwell, Ralphie, and Sweet Sunshine were discovered, I'd be totally in the doghouse!"

I finally get it! "So that's why the case is a secret. Your mom can't find out."

Misty explains, "I'll only be grounded until the next millennium." Her face starts to match the downward direction of Maxwell's floppy ears.

My detective genes (which I suspect I inherited from international super sleuth, Patch, my somewhere-in-the-universe-but-not-here-yet dad) are trying to figure out an angle here. "I'll need to spend a little time alone with the subject."

Misty backs away in awe. "Of course. Anything you say."

43

I move closer to Maxwell, who immediately hops away from me, burrowing himself deep inside his temporary home.

The Case Of Maxwell: The Depressed Orphan Bunny

IDENTIFYING DATA

SUBJECT: Maxwell (Last name unknown). Floppy ears, brown eyes, twitchy nose, off-white fur with black spots and a pink belly. Appears to be full grown. Exact age unknown.

NATURE OF CONTACT: Introduced by a new girl at Palmville Middle School named Misty Longfellow.

LENGTH OF CONTACT: Less than five minutes. Have yet to pet the subject at the time of this notation.

BACKGROUND MATERIAL: Subject lives in hiding, after having been rescued by Misty Longfellow, an avid animal lover. Is acting strange, even for a bunny. Refuses food and water. Remains statue still. Maintains a constant in-the-dumps attitude and expresses little to no interest in cheering up.

DIAGNOSTIC CATEGORY: Orphan Bunny Depression.

METHODS: More visits and observation.

A digital meditation bell rings on my PDA, signaling that it's Indigo inquiring about my whereabouts. I quickly text her back to tell her I'm on my way. After a quick good-bye to Misty, I hop on my bike and head down the winding canyon road, reversing the twisting and turning pathway home.

Misty rushes after me. "I'm beyond pleased that you've taken the case." She yelps like a wild dog, which inspires the neighborhood dogs to start howling again. Then a flock of small birds trail her as she trots back up the hill to check on her peculiar bunny.

I feel the dry wind against all the features of my face. My hair dances in every direction. I swipe in front of me to get a clear view of the dusty road that pours out onto Main Street. Then it hits me, almost as hard as the harsh reality that a math quiz is in my very near future. I've landed a new case! I wonder if this is how my super-sleuthing dad begins his new cases.

QUESTIONS: Would Patch have said yes to this case too? What are the first steps that he would take to get to the bottom of Mr. Maxwell's unusual behavior?

Frederick leaps onto my bed, carrying a fake bone that he madly shakes back and forth until it's totally blurry. I remind him, "Freddy Fred Frederick, you are not a dog." Not surprisingly, my words fall on deaf cat ears. Poor Frederick, that's why he doesn't have any furry feline friends. He's convinced he's a furry canine!

Frederick is about to curl up in a ball, the way a cat would do if he were to go to sleep, when his mood suddenly shifts. He starts sniffing my hands with great suspicion. He knows I've been with another animal! I quickly reassure him, "Frederick, it's just a forlorn bunny in need of some analysis. You're still my number one boy cat."

But Frederick has a different opinion of the situation. He decides to sleep on a heap of dirty clothes instead of my cozy bed tonight. While he broods in the corner, I insist, "Your favorite sleeping spot is still here if you change your mind."

I crawl under my swirly pink paisley sheets, take out

my PDA, and press the on button. Immediately, a loud pop tune blasts from the pint-size troll speakers. I quickly turn down the volume, careful not to alert my always on-duty mother to the fact that I'm still up. With the sound muted now, I input my data about today's wild ride.

Then I decide to respond to Amy's e-mail message from earlier this afternoon.

> To: mememe@palmville.net
> From: pavatar@palmville.net
>
> I never knew that you and mathematics were
> such "good friends." I wish I could say the
> same. That particular subject and I are not
> even close to being casual acquaintances. I
> haven't been able to open a book since the
> last school bell. The new case is proving to
> be intriguing. I've decided to call it "The Case
> of Maxwell: The Depressed Orphan Bunny."
> Please keep this important detail to yourself.
> I only revealed it to you because you're my
> best friend and best friends know how to

 47

keep secrets, and of course as inspiration for
the new look that you're designing for me. :)!
Portia

P.S. Not sure stripes are my thing.

I'm just about to shut down when I notice the reminder
I had left on my PDA from early this morning.

REMINDER: Find your missing father!

It's a fact that no matter what kind of day I'm having,
each night I work hard to stay on track and review the
case of a lifetime, "The Case of Patch, My Missing Father:
A Man of Many Hats." Now that I have taken on the
Maxwell case, I'll have to work extra hard on the search
to find my father.

A solitary bird sings a sweet song in the darkness
outside my window. This nature melody fills the warm,
starry night. I close my eyes and try to imagine my father,
Patch, for the trillionth time, reminding myself that the
world cannot be that big a place. The universe is filled

48

with much bigger planets than Earth, like Saturn and Jupiter, for example. Here, on our home planet, there are definitely ways to find people, especially traveling and long-lost fathers.

Chapter 6

It's morning, and I find Frederick back on the bed, resting against my feet, having returned to his favorite sleeping spot. He slowly lifts his head and sniffs the air. It appears that he's going to give me a second chance, but then he dramatically leaps off the bed, rushing around, seriously scoping out all the corners of the room. But all he finds are dust bunnies, not a real one named Maxwell. I tell him, "I promise to spend more time with you. I just need to conquer the subject of mathematics, rescue a living thing in need, and find the father I have never known. You'll see. I'll have mountains of time soon."

The telephone rings downstairs. I hear Indigo laugh at the top of her lungs. I know exactly who is on the other end of the phone line. After what seems to be an hour of excited high-pitched teenage-sounding squeals, Indigo rings the wind chimes. That's the Avatar signal that breakfast is ready. I gather my textbooks in my arms, careful not to forget the one entitled Mathematics: Applications and Connections. Frederick swipes at my polka-dotted shoelaces, trying to prevent me from heading out the door. I put down my books and gently hold his head between my hands, reminding him that I've got to go to school, which I know saddens him. He looks up at me with his irresistible puppy/kitty cat eyes, sending me the message loud and clear that he'll miss me while I toil away at integers, fractals, and other mathematical challenges.

7:43 A.M., AVATAR KITCHEN

Indigo flutters around the kitchen, putting the final touches on a pomegranate-inspired breakfast. She appears to have butterfly wings attached to her back as she whirls through this morning's breakfast preparation. After a few minutes, she places a heap of pomegranate scramble onto my wobbly clay plate. I manage a smile, staring at the sweet mixture that awaits me. She watches me take the first bite, but I know her mind is somewhere else. She declares, "Rock has been out in the canyons all night fighting the fires. He's exhausted! I'm going to prepare a pick-me-up treat for him, and then we'll be ready to go."

I am curious, so I ask, "What's the latest news about the fires? I can still smell smoke coming from the canyons."

"Rock will be at the station all day today. You know you're always welcome to stop by on your way home from school and ask him yourself."

Without thinking once, twice, or even three times about it, I respond, "I'm way too busy. I've got a new case."

Indigo stops what she's doing and turns to me. "Have you been holding out on me?"

"I took it on yesterday. It's highly confidential. All I can say is that it involves the new girl, Misty Longfellow, and a mysterious friend of hers."

"How exciting. An opportunity to grow!"

I then tell Indigo a little bit more about Misty's wayward

animals and the insect orphans she rescues on a daily basis. Indigo listens to my tale as she slices one of our garden's ripe red tomatoes, just a fraction of the many fresh ingredients she has gathered for Rock's mega-sandwich-to-go. Frederick, meanwhile, circles my feet, playing a game with me, trying to see if I'll pick him up or not. I'm careful to pay extra attention to him since his little episode last night, so I pick him up and place him on my lap. He wraps himself in a ball, purring away, savoring this honey-sweetened moment.

Indigo looks up at the wall clock, then at me. "Hurry, Portia! You're going to be late for school!" She quickly wraps up Rock's surprise package, mumbling to herself, "Grilled eggplant, black bean hummus, goat cheese puffs with lavender, and fig crisps. I just know I'm forgetting something."

7:56 A.M., PALMVILLE STREET

It's not until we're in our burnt orange hybrid rolling down the street that Indigo remembers what she forgot: my lunch! She hands me ten dollars.

IMPORTANT NOTE: This is a highly momentous occasion. I am given lunch money for the first time in my entire school career, which means I'll have free rein over my lunchtime nourishment! My mind drifts to thoughts of chili cheese fries, strawberry ice cream, and an extra gooey mud pie.

While looking out the window watching my neighbors begin their day, I quietly celebrate this accidental stroke of luck. Even though there's a giant yellow cloud blocking the sun from making a proper entrance today, a visual effect brought to us from the out-of-control wildfires, my outlook is sunny. I think to myself that maybe things are going to change around here now.

Chapter 7

I page through my math worksheets in preparation for that thrilling moment when Miss Killjoy's joyless pop quiz finally arrives. Then I feel a tap on my shoulder and hear, "Miss Avatar, are you ready?"

Startled and more than a little bit surprised to see Webster standing there, I ask, "For what?"

"For the imminent math quiz that awaits us."

"Not exactly."

Webster then boldly sits down next to me. "Do you need any help?"

Is this really happening? Neptune to Portia. Am I

in a movie or is this cute nerd boy sharing his personal space with me and offering to share a portion of his left brain, too?

NOTE: Sometimes I think I actually have a crush on Webster, but I'm not sure. I've discussed the matter with Amy, who is convinced that it's just a momentary lapse in sanity, which I will grow out of as soon as I meet a more crush-worthy candidate or start eighth grade, whichever comes first.

Before I have time for a private tutorial from W.H., A.C. steps into the picture, waving a letter-size color pencil sketch of a potential girl detective outfit in my face. She announces, "I've done it again! Your new look will send a fashion buzz across the country. It's positively electric." She looks over at Webster, while still talking to me, "Am I interrupting something?"

I quickly jump in, "We were just talking."

Webster adds, "About math."

Amy winks at him, then finds a seat between us, ignoring the fact that Webster and I were engaged in a conversation. "I've been thinking that your new look needs to make a statement that says, 'I see everything, but reveal nothing.'" She shows me one drawing of a pair of pants that has pockets sewn inside and outside. There are so many pockets that I can barely tell what color she has chosen for the pants. She continues, "The pockets are for the evidence."

I check out the sketch and think that even though I do sometimes find bits of evidence that would fit inside a pocket, my real findings are filed in my brain. They are thoughts about the people—or in the case of Maxwell, about bunnies—who are in need of being figured out or who have lost their way.

My thoughts are interrupted by the sound of Misty's voice. I look up and there she is, swinging her opened pendant in front of me. Excitedly, she screeches, "Sweet Sunshine! She's gone. I've lost her!"

Thinking on my feet, even though I'm still sitting down, I ask, "Where did you see her last?"

"At The—"

I finish her sentence, "Tent!"

Amy looks up at Misty. "Excuse us, but Portia and I are focusing on serious business here."

Misty insists, "This is about a missing cricket with only three legs. I'd say that's pretty serious." She sighs. "How will she ever survive without me?"

Amy just shakes her head in an "I told you so" sort of way, slipping her fashion sketch into the center of her pop-star-emblazoned homework folder. "Portia, text me when you're ready to get serious about beautification."

Caught in the middle, all I can do is just nod okay. In an attempt to escape this tense girl triangle, I take out my PDA to make a few quick notes.

OBSERVATION: Amy and Misty appear to be from different planets, both of which are currently circling the same galaxy, and unless I figure out a solution soon, they are about to collide!

I look over at the spot where Webster was sitting, but he's gone. The first bell rings, and I think I see him caught in the swell of kids rushing to avoid the late bell. With one deep breath, I scoop up my books and zoom in through the front door, careening down the hallway, speed-walking in the direction of Mr. Scuzzy's Media for the Millennium class. Amy is way ahead of me, while Misty, who has a highly tuned radar for what seems to be my every move, is right beside me. "Portia, we've got to find him!"

I stop my furious pace and decide to listen to what Misty has to say. "I'm all ears."

"Did anyone ever tell you that you're an excellent listener?"

"Thanks—that's not something I hear a lot. Misty, I've never actually been late for class, so do you think you could tell me what you have to say now?"

"Oh, there I go. Talking, talking, talking." Misty just barely keeps up with me. She confesses, "Every time I rescue a helpless animal, something always goes wrong. Look what's happened to Sweet Sunshine!"

Trying to find a way to help Misty's current stressed-out state of being while still trying to get to Mr. Scuzzy's class on time, I insist, "I'm going to find her. She's at The Tent for sure."

Misty admits, "The worst part of my extreme love of animals is that they are usually wild and untamed, which makes for highly unpredictable behavior. I can never guess what's going to happen next, and that always creates some sort of big mess."

The second bell rings. We are now both officially late for Mr. Scuzzy's class. Running at Olympic speed, I reassure Misty, "I just know we're going to find Sweet Sunshine."

Interestingly, Misty doesn't seem to care in the least that she's late for class. In fact, she's bursting with intergalactic enthusiasm now that she knows I'll be helping her find her beloved cricket. If she had wings right now, she'd be flying.

> **FACT:** By agreeing to listen to Misty's unhappy story about Sweet Sunshine, I've broken a highly punishable school rule. I'm late!

I offer Mr. Scuzzy the legitimate-sounding excuse that I was helping the new girl find her way to the classroom. He buys 74 percent of my story, so he gives me and Misty a simple warning. My nerves are on fire from this unprecedented transgression in my otherwise perfect school record. Amy just smirks at me as I settle into my seat, then rolls her eyes in Misty's direction.

After class, Amy breezes by me while I make plans with Misty to meet at The Tent right after school to search for Sweet Sunshine. Misty cheers at the prospect of working together on a rescue.

Then I casually inquire about progress with Maxwell. Misty covers her mouth and gasps. "I was so wrapped up in Sweet Sunshine's disappearance, I forgot to check on him this morning! I've completely abandoned poor Maxwell! Could we possibly switch our meeting at The Tent until later?"

"I'll be there studying all afternoon."

"Coolio! I promise to give you a full report on Maxwell when I see you."

Misty is almost out the door when I offer, "Look for any unusual signs. Something that appears out of the ordinary."

"For sure! I'll totally look out for any signs of unusualness." Misty leaves the building, galloping home to collect more evidence for the case.

I begin my all-too-familiar walk to The Tent from school. Sometimes I play a game where I close my eyes and take long strides down the hill in total darkness. I try it today just for fun. I shut my eyes and get pretty far down the hill until a wild parrot squawks overhead, interrupting my concentration. I follow him as he leads me to a shaded spot under a grouping of palms. I curl up into a comfortable position, the way Frederick does just before he goes to sleep on my bed (when he's not mad at me). The faint sound of a fire truck fills the still dry air as I open my PDA to input the new data from today.

3:15 P.M.,
UNDER A PALMVILLE PALM

I reflect on the case so far, wondering if there's a connection between Maxwell's atypical bunny behavior and Sweet Sunshine's recent escape.

That's when I realize that this new case doesn't star Maxwell, the super sad bunny. And Sweet Sunshine isn't the lead subject either. It's Misty, the animal-loving new girl! There's a definite unsolved mystery that lies beneath her extreme behavior that needs figuring out.

IMPORTANT QUESTION: Why is Misty so rescue crazy?

FACT: It's a noble cause to save animals from dangerous situations. However, it appears that Misty's steady stream of rescues prevent her from having a normal middle school existence.

The Case of Misty Longfellow: The Mystifying Animal Rescuer

IDENTIFYING DATA

SUBJECT: Misty Longfellow (aka New Girl). Twelve years old. A recent import to Palmville. Straight brown hair, usually worn with a part down the middle, tucked behind her ears. Big, round, hazel eyes. Wire-rimmed spectacles that have seen happier days. Purple-tinted hardware on all her teeth. Is highly excitable. Appears to have a warm heart, expressed mainly when it comes to helpless creatures of all types and breeds.

NATURE OF CONTACT: Made a memorable first impression in Miss Killjoy's class.

LENGTH OF CONTACT: Approximately twenty-four hours.

BACKGROUND MATERIAL: Subject is known to rescue stray and wounded animals without blinking. Lives deep in the dusty canyons.

DIAGNOSTIC CATEGORY: Chronic Animal Rescuer.

METHODS: Spend time with subject and observe her perplexing behavior.

Misty mustn't know that the new case is actually about her. With one press of an onscreen button, my secret data is saved and stored. I look up, expecting to see the sun blazing down on me, but instead, it's Webster H.!

NOTE: Webster appears to be popping up a lot lately!

QUESTION: Could this be a coincidence, or is it an unknown and bewildering boy pattern worth investigating?

Webster awkwardly begins the conversation. "Are you studying for the quiz? I have determined with 100 percent probability that it will occur tomorrow."

Carefully placing my PDA inside the secret pocket of my knapsack, acting as naturally as possible, I make a move to stand up. I respond casually, "Just taking some notes."

Like Prince Charming (if he was eleven and a half), Webster reaches for my hand. "Allow me, Miss Avatar. Where are you headed?"

Without thinking about it, I give him my hand, and suddenly I'm vertical. I look at Webster and simply say, "Contentment."

Webster freezes, then asks, "Are you referring to the state of being when one is extremely at ease in one's situation?"

"Contentment is my mom's vegetarian restaurant on Main Street. I'm going to be late."

"I understand." With an outstretched arm, his right hand points in the direction of Main Street. "To Contentment!"

RANDOM QUESTIONS: Why Webster's sudden interest in spending time with me? What exactly is that burning question he wanted to ask me when we last met in the canyons?

I look at myself from an aerial view. Having a boy walk me all the way to Main Street is not something I planned. Throughout the entire journey, I'm church-mouse quiet, not sharing even one noun, verb, or adjective with him. We make it to The Tent in record time, thanks to the high-speed pace I set the whole way there. Outside The Tent, I find myself staring at the front entrance. Webster comments on the antique bell, made from a carved horseshoe, that hangs at the center of the door. "Fascinating, indeed!"

Trying hard to avoid even one uncomfortable boy/girl moment, I smile. "It's different."

Webster then makes an about-face and steps down the three small steps to the sidewalk. I follow him and catch his hand. "Was there something you wanted to ask me?"

We both look down at our intertwined hands. I gracefully slip mine away, cleverly turning it into a wave.

Webster attempts to say something but can't get the words out. Then, just like that, he's gone.

QUESTION: Why is it that boys are even more confusing than middle school math?

ANOTHER QUESTION: What is the formula for staying cool while in the presence of a boy you might like just a little bit?

Chapter 8

The Pythagorean Theorem
In any right triangle, the square of the length
of the hypotenuse is equal to the sum of the
squares of the lengths of the other two sides.
The hypotenuse is the side of a right triangle
that is opposite the right angle.

Who came up with this theorem? I really want to meet him. I have a few important questions I'd like answered.

While waiting for Misty, I toil away at homework at my favorite corner table. I decide to take a break from triangles and right angles to picture the new outfit that will be conceived and designed by none other than Amy Clamdigger.

When it comes to girl detective fashion, I need to be comfortable while still maintaining an air of mystery. The comfort part of the outfit is necessary, in case I am required to run long distances, lift heavy objects, or crawl into dark caves (or maybe a bunny hut!). To achieve the appearance of mystery, it will have to be all about the hat. The hat will set the look, and the rest of the fashion statement will follow from there. I make a note to tell Amy about this detective accessory insight.

But she's three steps ahead of me. According to my PDA, an e-mail from one Miss Amy Clamdigger arrived less than fifteen seconds ago. I click on the blinking icon to see what news she brings me this afternoon.

To: pavatar@palmville.net
From: mememe@palmville.net

I know you meant to text me, so I forgive you in advance. No apologies necessary. ;) I was

browsing the Palmville boutiques this afternoon, scouring the racks for inspiration. Of
course I found it, but first things first. What
is up between you and Webster? I witnessed
you two walking through town together. You
weren't on a date, were you? No way! That
just wouldn't add up. Anyway, back to my
inspiration. I see you in pink. Pink has got to
play a role in the outfit in some way. Hold
everything! My creativity is bouncing off the
walls right now. I've got to take a beauty nap
immediately! I must get my rest before another
rendezvous with my "new friend" later.
Truffles and tiaras, Amy

I immediately respond to Amy's message.

To: mememe@palmville.net
From: pavatar@palmville.net

Thanks for working on my new look. I was
thinking about the sketch, and maybe we

should mellow out on the pockets. As a
detective, I need to be more discreet about
where I store my evidence. Peace, Portia

P.S. Who is your new friend?

A response from Amy arrives in a matter of seconds.

To: pavatar@palmville.net
From: mememe@palmville.net

Note taken. BTW, meet me at the Purple
Haze Boutique off Main on Glenside Drive
tomorrow after school. There's something
I want to show you. For now, I'm going
to close my eyes and take my beauty
nap. It's important for the balance of my
inner and outer well-being. Laughter and
lollipops, Amy

P.S. The true identity of my new friend will
remain confidential until further notice.

P.P.S. I hear Miss Killjoy's quiz counts for more than half of our grade. You're not worried about it, are you? It's the last thing on my mind. I don't have a clue why I even brought it up.

Of course I'm worried about the upcoming math quiz!

QUESTIONS: Why does Amy have to remind me about this fact when we were in the middle of creating my new image? And what's the big mystery about her "friend"? Who could this person be?

Then I get another message from Amy.

To: pavatar@palmville.net
From: mememe@palmville.net

I forgot to warn you. Beware of the animal kingdom. A friendship with insect-loving

new girl will only lead to fleas. Paging
your favorite laundry detergent! ;) Ame

OBSERVATION: Amy seems to be extra concerned
about me spending time with Misty.

I decide to take a moment to remember how much
Amy means to me and make a note to explain to her that
my relationship with Misty is purely professional and an
opportunity to perfect my detective skills.

I then focus my attention on other pressing matters.
It's time to study for math, especially because Misty
will be here any minute. I find it difficult to focus on
the intricate art of mathematics, and so my thoughts drift
to the type of hat that will serve as the perfect accent to
my upcoming new look. Sun, baseball, floppy, beanie,
knitted, cotton, velveteen, skateboard, denim, camou-
flage, Hawaiian, a scarf, or maybe it'll be a beret.

The reason I'm so convinced that it will be the hat
that will complete my outfit for the new case is because
my traveling father, who has somehow managed to miss

the Palmville exit on his way to saving the world from one international disaster after another, always wears a different hat for his cases. I cannot confirm this for sure, because it's just a theory, but I know in my heart that I share this same detective trait.

I then reach for my math book, but what I see is Indigo slowly sliding a plate of pomegranate linguini in front of me. It's her newest creation, part of a growing list of pomegranate productions brought to us (me!) by Indigo and Hap. She stares down at me and, in a sincere mother voice, says, "I want your honest opinion." Hap stands behind her, nodding in agreement. She continues, "It's one of our most promising contenders for the new spring menu. I'm even thinking of featuring it as an entree." She stops herself. "Of course, I'm not trying to influence you in any way."

Two sets of eyes stare me down while I wrap the linguini around my fork, a technique that Indigo taught me back when I was in kindergarten. Carefully I chew on the soft, noodly potential entree. Why do I feel like an animal stuck in a cage, with scientists seriously lacking in social skills examining my every move? To make my performance more believable, I close my eyes as I chew. Then I come up with this: "It's definitely on the right track. I mean, it's edible, but not incredible—yet."

Indigo lets out a sigh of relief but pushes hard for more positive feedback. "So you like it?"

Hap sneaks a few words in to congratulate Indigo. "You've done it again!" With a movie-star twinkle in his eye, he blurts out, "Indeed an accomplishment!"

Then it's hushed silence as I take another bite. Still chewing, I offer, "Maybe it's a little tart?"

Indigo listens intently, reviewing all the ingredients in her mind. "Got it." She turns to Hap. "We must rethink our lemon infusion!"

Hap is so thrilled that Indigo has included him in the collaboration that he does a backflip in his brain. "Absolutely!" He rushes to the kitchen, eager to make up a new batch of Contentment's very own brand of pomegranate linguini.

Indigo leans over to me. "A peanut butter and raspberry jam sandwich coming right up." Her organic cotton ankle-length flowing skirt swirls as she heads toward the kitchen. When she's halfway there, she turns to me with a peculiar look on her face. "Did you hear that? There's a chirping sound coming from the latest shipment of wild oats."

Playing it dumb with a capital D, I respond, "I don't know what you mean. I didn't hear anything."

"Odd, it sounded distinctly like a cricket."

Hiding any sign of alarm, I insist, "No way. It's not even close to cricket season!"

Indigo is thankfully more concerned with how to feature pomegranate on her new menu than she is with figuring out my logic, which is not very "logical." I know exactly who is chirping in the pile of oats. On cue, an urgent message from Misty arrives in my PDA's in-box.

To: pavatar@palmville.net
From: animalsrule@palmville.net

Please don't hate me! I'm on my way. I
was trying to calm Maxwell's nerves this
whole time. He's acting even more bizarro.

Infinite unusualness abounds! I've tried to make mental notes of everything. Maybe there's a clue somewhere in there for you to pursue.

I quickly text her back.

To: animalsrule@palmville.net
From: pavatar@palmville.net

She's here!

A new text message flies into my PDA at the speed of digital lightning.

To: pavatar@palmville.net
From: animalsrule@palmville.net

Where?

My fingers type fast, faster, fastest.

To: animalsrule@pallmville.net

From: pavatar@palmville.net

Sweet Sunshine is residing in the oats. She
must have popped out when you introduced
her to me!

No response. Then I get an urgent message.

To: pavatar@palmville.net

From: animalsrule@palmville.net

I told my mom that we would be studying for
math together until dinner. Are you cool with
my minor deception? I hope so, because I'm
right outside now.

Misty rushes in through the beaded entrance. At full
volume, she announces, "We've only got thirty minutes to
find Sweet Sunshine!"

A handful of customers at the other tables turn

to look at who is behind this thundering declaration. I whisk Misty off to the counter near the bag of oats where Sweet Sunshine is hiding out, smiling at The Tent's diners and my mom along the way. Indigo whispers to me as I pass by her, "You're not going to let your case get in the way of your studying, are you?"

Thinking quickly, a required skill for any detective, I say, "We are studying. We're taking a break."

"But didn't Misty just get here?"

"Mom, our collective brains are on math overload. We need a whole grain snack to restore our brain cells so we can properly concentrate."

Thankfully, Hap calls Indigo back into the kitchen to review tonight's specials. Misty and I take full advantage of the opportunity to find Sweet Sunshine!

FIFTEEN MINUTES LATER

There's no sign of Sweet Sunshine anywhere. Not even a chirp. Indigo has checked in on us every five minutes, so that hasn't helped our search either. And now Mrs. Longfellow is on her way over to The Tent to pick up Misty. We've accomplished exactly nothing. To add to this unsuccessful mission, neither of us has studied for the impending math quiz.

6:43 P.M.,

OUTSIDE CONTENTMENT (THE TENT)

Misty and I sit on the hand-carved Indian bench and wait for Mrs. Longfellow under the starry night. I look at Misty, defeated. "Killjoy is going to kill us!"

Misty agrees. "A lost cricket is a terrible excuse for not studying. Oh, gee, I did it again! I'm so incredibly sorry, Portia Avatar: Girl Psychoanalytic Detective." Tears fill her round hazel eyes. "What's wrong with me?"

This is a chance to pursue the case a little further to determine why Misty gets so overly involved with her subjects, but I decide it's more important to just be her friend right now. "I promise to keep looking for Sweet Sunshine. Let's make a pact that we won't give up until the three-legged cricket is finally found."

Misty looks up at me, hopeful for the first time in more than twenty-nine minutes. She leaps to her feet. "Sweet Sunshine couldn't have gotten lost in a better place! With your watchful eye and all the oats, fresh fruit, and raw vegetables she can eat, it'll be like a bug spa retreat. She won't ever want to come home!"

Mrs. Longfellow pulls up in her shiny station wagon and doesn't bother to say hello. She seems to be in a big rush and appears to be very low on patience. She shouts to Misty through the opened passenger-side window, "Get in the car!"

Misty quickly jumps in. As the car starts to pull away into the Palmville night, she shouts, "I'm so pleased you're my new friend."

"Thanks, Misty." Mrs. L. doesn't even wait long enough for me to wish Misty a good night.

I sit back on the bench and look up at the expansive universe above me and wonder what tomorrow will bring. Today was a grab bag of surprises. I break out laughing when I think about how Webster and I held hands for almost five seconds! I catch myself, straightening out my hair, looking at the passersby from the corner of my eye, making sure no one witnessed my momentary slip.

I take a long pause and silently ask the glittery bursts of energy overhead to work together with me tomorrow when I sit in Killjoy's class facing a letter-size sheet of white paper covered with triangular shapes and unfamiliar combinations of numerals. I ask the moon that is on its way to utter fullness to please keep Sweet Sunshine safe tonight and let tomorrow be the day when Misty and I finally find her. I make a promise with our neighboring planets to remind Amy C. that our friendship is exactly the same today as it was yesterday and the day before, too. Then I make a special request to the entire Milky Way galaxy to please let Frederick forgive me for spending so much time away from home and for not playing fetch or rubbing his belly or sneaking him a spoonful of his favorite canned cat food.

Frederick sleeps in the far corner of my room again, closing his eyes, pretending that my dirty laundry pile is more comfortable than my fluffy purple down comforter. I sit up, propped by an extra stash of round velvet toss pillows, staring at my open math textbook. Sample formulas and equations on worksheets are spread out everywhere. Miraculously, I manage to get through two practice quizzes and feel 55.6 percent ready for tomorrow, which will in all likelihood be the day that Killjoy will bestow the quiz upon our math class.

Like I do most every night, I wash my face with mind-expanding mango and kiwi blend and then slip under the covers. As I prepare for sleep, I find myself creating my own theorem.

Portia Avatar's Theorem
There is exactly one mother, one cat, and one
daughter, the sum of which equals the current

makeup of the Avatar home. If one father, whose name is Patch, only knew how important his presence in this current incomplete formula would be and how it would lead to maximum happiness, then he would with 100 percent certainty grab the next plane, hop the next train, or catch the next bus to Palmville, USA.

Chapter 9

Media for the Millennium is in progress. The discussion this morning is on media and our absorbent minds. Mr. Scuzzy, who wears his usual black T-shirt and faded jeans accompanied by a pair of original Converse All Stars, is midway through a description of what the brain looks like when it discovers something new. I feel a tap on my shoulder halfway through Scuzzy's next sentence about programming our internal circuitry. Then a note drops onto my lap.

Maxwell hasn't touched his food in
twenty-four hours, but he's getting bigger!
It doesn't make sense. He needs another
visit from a professional (aka you!).
Any news on my Sweet Sunshine?
Your newest best friend,
Misty

Mr. Scuzzy appears from out of nowhere, looking down
at me with a disappointed look on his face. All I can manage
is a very weak, "Hi, Mr. S. Nice weather, isn't it?"

"It's fire season and unseasonably hot."

"I see your point."

Staring at Misty's handwritten note, which she wrote
on bright purple stationery (did she have to be obvious
about it?), he gestures for me to hand over the evidence.
Because he's a teacher on the cool side, he doesn't read
the note out loud. But because he's a teacher, he requests
my presence (and Misty's, too) after school.

When the bell rings, Amy brushes by me. She
whispers to me like she's telling me a really big secret,

"Check your book bag." On my way out the door, I reach into the outer pocket of my bag and discover another handwritten note. This one was scribbled quickly on a torn piece of graph paper.

Well, I guess we'll be rescheduling our boutique visit for tomorrow. BTW, from one close friend to another: malaria, yellow fever, the plague? I told you, P. Stay away from new girl. Stay far away! Do you even know what you're getting into?

9:03 A.M., STUDY HALL, PALMVILLE MIDDLE SCHOOL

Safely inside study hall with twenty-three minutes of "study" time ahead of me, I jot down a few more notes about the early and yet significant developments of this mystifying case, starring Miss Longfellow, before preparing for the imminent math quiz.

RECENT FACTS SURROUNDING MISTY'S CASE:

1. Misty continues to think about her animal friends 24/7.
2. Misty is an amateur at passing notes.

2:35 P.M., MATH CLASS, PALMVILLE MIDDLE SCHOOL

IMPORTANT NEWS: No math quiz today!

When the bell rings at the end of Miss Killjoy's class, Webster scratches his head, completely stumped by his miscalculation. I come up to him to say hi, but he's too busy inputting number combinations into his supersonic calculator to notice that I exist. It's as if we've never held hands!

FACT: Boys are seriously unpredictable.

Mr. Scuzzy circles around me and Misty, who sit like cowgirls in an old Western, tied to a tree with a flaming fire just below our feet. I can feel small beads of sweat form around my forehead. It is unseasonably hot! Maybe the fires just outside town have something to do with that fact. I decide to clasp my hands together and place them on top of the desk, pulling out all the "I am really a good girl who never gets into trouble" stops. Mr. S. falls for my performance, because he spends only three minutes on a mini-lecture about respecting others and the value of paying attention in class. He finally steps up to the front of the room and leans against his desk, folding his arms across his chest. He looks first at Misty and then at me. He proclaims, "I'm going to give you ladies a challenge."

I hold my tongue, knowing that it's after school,

which means the in-classroom rule about speaking up without raising your hand is even more strictly enforced. I keep my mouth shut, but my hand shoots up. Mr. Scuzzy motions for me to speak. I begin, "I'm all about challenges, Mr. S."

Misty leaps up. "Me too!" She looks at me for approval, but I ignore her, for fear of another after-school lecture from Mr. Scuzzy.

Mr. Scuzzy explains the challenge. "I'd like you both to write a short essay about second chances. It's your second chance to make up for today, and you may even earn bonus points, if you wow me."

When Mr. S. gives us the final okay to leave, I am ultra polite. I collect my belongings and slowly make my way out the door. As soon as the door is closed behind me, I race outside to freedom. Misty jogs up beside me. "Isn't Mr. Scuzzy so handsome? And we might even get extra points! That is just totally awesome of him!"

"Misty, Mr. S. just gave us extra work to do on top of all our other homework. And there's still the random pop quiz coming any day now in Miss Killjoy's class."

"That is so correct! What was I thinking? You are so wise, P. Avatar. Can we go find Sweet Sunshine now?"

FACT: I am annoyed with Misty's overeager personality right now!

QUESTIONS: Maybe Amy's warnings were right. Maybe new girl is trouble with a capital T. Or could it be that Misty tries too hard? Is she just new at this whole friendship thing and so doesn't know how to act like a normal kid who has been practicing the art of friendship since before kindergarten?

I decide to be professional, stick my emotions in my back pocket, and stay on track with the case. Trying to remain cool, even though my internal thermometer is about to burst, I insist, "I need to make one stop first. Vera is counting on my help with the new shipment of lamp shades."

Misty sits down on the sidewalk, with her hands clasped over her head. "It's me, isn't it?"

"No Misty, Vera Alloway is truly waiting for me!"

"Who is Vera? Can I meet her? I won't be a bother."

 91

"It'll just be for a minute."

Misty brightens like the morning sun. Her practical leather ready-for-rain-and-shine sandals are now solidly on the ground. "You actually mean you're going to continue speaking to me even after I severely got you in trouble?"

I remind her, "It's for the case, Misty."

Embarrassed, she meekly responds, "Of course, the case. For sure, it's for the case."

Finally picking up on the fact that I'm not feeling immensely talkative, Misty slows down the speed of her chatter. Silence passes between us until we get to the entrance of Trash and Treasures.

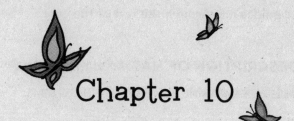

Chapter 10

I open the front door to Trash and Treasures and make my way past the overflowing shelves and racks of torn mink coats, pointy party shoes, worn-out suede jackets, saggy sofas, and chipped flower vases. Misty walks around with her head turning in all directions at once, soaking up the unusualness of Vera's magnificent interior junk festival.

Misty then gasps in astonishment as she scoops up something incredibly special. It's a hat! It was sitting there all by itself, balancing between two racks of donated Halloween costumes. It's got "girl detective" written all over it. She hands me this precious new discovery. I place it on my head. It fits perfectly. I declare, "This will be the hat that guides me through the rest of the case!"

DESCRIPTION OF HAT: A plaid newsboy hat in all shades of pink with white, red, yellow, and a touch of brown.

QUESTION: How did Misty know that I was looking for a new hat for the case?

FRIENDSHIP RULE #2: True friends surprise you when you least expect it.

Where is a mirror in this junk palace? I weed through piles of dated encyclopedias and used paperback dictionaries. I don't find a single mirror, but I discover the lamp shade shipment untouched. I've got to find Vera to ask about the price tag of this stupendous chapeau and see if I can postpone my assistance with the lamp shades for another day. "Paging Vera Alloway? If you can hear me, please give me a sign."

Nothing.

I go back to my hunt for a mirror. As I weave through this highly disorganized dust palace, I turn around, and there's Vera holding an antique hand mirror with a tarnished silver frame and handle. She casually comments, "Nice hat."

OBSERVATION: Vera always knows what I'm thinking. She *is* a mind reader.

She continues, "It's yours," and hands me the mirror, which looks like its previous owner was a pampered princess out of a colorful fairy tale.

I take a long look at the hat. "I love it! It's just what I need for my new case."

Then Misty pops up from behind a rolling rack of Hawaiian shirts. "Hi, Vera Alloway. I'm Misty Longfellow!"

Vera extends her hand for a hearty shake. "So you're the mysterious new girl in town."

Misty is all smiles. "Portia told you about me?"

Vera rests her arm on the saddle of a lopsided gold-plated carousel horse and asks Misty, "How's progress on the case?"

Misty confesses, "It's all my fault. Now we've got to find Sweet Sunshine, and then there's Maxwell, who is definitely not doing well at all."

I step in. "Vera, do you mind if I hold off on helping you with the lamp shades today? The case has sprouted a new micro-mystery in the form of a three-legged cricket."

Vera lets out a belly laugh that fills the cluttered room. She looks me in the eye, almost as if she's an eye doctor about to check if I need glasses or not. "The lamp shades can wait; sounds like the cricket can't!"

Vera notices Misty admiring a few faded postcards. "Take them. They're yours."

Misty leaps up like a cheerleader. "A gift?"

"Enjoy!" Then Vera calls me aside with some advice. "Stay on track. Follow all leads and remember to listen. That's how you'll solve this one."

I want to explain to Vera that the case is not about creatures in peril anymore, but instead it's about Misty herself. I whisper, "Everything has changed."

Vera is now ushering me out the door, with Misty close behind me. She smiles. "Nothing ever stays the same. That's one of the biggest rules that the universe has to offer us."

Chapter 11

5:56 P.M.,
CONTENTMENT (THE TENT)

Misty and I dump our book bags at "my" table. Misty takes out the old postcards she's just received from Vera and begins to examine them. Indigo joins us, carrying a book entitled *The Peculiar Pomegranate*.

NOTE: Even though Indigo has been cooking food and inventing recipes for all of her adult life, she never stops studying the art of food creation.

QUESTION: I wonder if I'll be an eternal student of something I love and follow in her determined-to-learn-something-new-every-day footsteps.

Hap nervously approaches Indigo with a plate of misshapen pomegranates. Indigo slowly and meticulously examines each piece of fruit. Finally she says, "These are great picks, Hap. I think we'll be able to work with all of them. Just keep them here for now. I need to taste a few before we start cooking. I'll meet you back in the kitchen in a few minutes."

Hap looks relieved and grins. "Right, Indigo. I'll be there! Waiting."

QUESTION: If someone waits long enough, does love eventually show up? Is love just about timing, or is there a mathematical formula for finding it?

Misty's mom calls her on her cell phone. Misty excuses herself from the table to quickly explain her whereabouts to Mrs. L., leaving her postcards on the table. I take out my math textbook to give the impression that I'm studying for the infamous pop quiz, while I slide Misty's postcards in a random spot in the book for safekeeping.

Indigo's probing eyes distract me from my "studying." She takes a sip from her hand-painted mug of chamomile tea, then squints at me. "There's something different about you. Can I have a clue?"

I tap my head. "The hat."

"Of course! It's wonderful, and it brings out your beautiful brown eyes. Where did you find such a delightful hat?"

"Misty found it at Trash and Treasures. And Vera gave it to me." While Indigo talks to me, she slices into one of the pomegranates that Hap has just delivered to her. I hear a chirping sound and freeze. My thoughts speed forward and land on one clear and distinct image. It's of a three-legged cricket named Sweet Sunshine. "Mom! Stop! Spare Sweet Sunshine, for Misty's sake! Every cricket deserves to live a rich and full life!"

Continuing with the forward motion of her slice, Indigo asks with a perplexed look on her face, "What are you talking about?"

"Stop, please. Listen!" The chirping picks up speed and intensity. Sweet Sunshine suddenly appears from the hidden side of the pomegranate. "We've got to save her! She's one of Misty's rescues!"

Indigo backs up off her chair, sending it flying across the room as I calmly coax Sweet Sunshine onto my left forefinger, cupping her with my right hand so she doesn't hop away. With keen mother instincts, Indigo is already in the kitchen, searching for a container that will serve as Sweet Sunshine's temporary home. In a flash, my super-heroine-rescuing-mother arrives back at the table. She hands me an old soy mayonnaise jar with a few strategic airholes punched into the metal cover. I carefully place my hand inside with Sweet Sunshine hanging on, totally confused about who I am and what I'm doing. She proceeds to test my patience meter until finally she decides she's ready to hop off my finger and into her new home away from home.

Indigo and I hug each other, celebrating our victorious rescue. She bursts out, "This calls for a papaya and pomegranate chilled salad. Let's see if I have any left in the kitchen!"

I hold the jar up close to my eyes and say, "Sweet Sunshine, even though you have an itsy-bitsy brain, I hope you understand that you're safe now. You will be seeing Misty as soon as she gets off the phone with her mother." I carefully walk outside with Sweet Sunshine inside the industrial-size jar to tell Misty the big news!

OBSERVATION: It's fun to save a living thing from danger. I'm starting to see why Misty is such a rescue freak.

IMPORTANT FACT: Since taking on this case, I have discovered that Misty and I have a few things in common, like being proud members of the mutual appreciation society of the animal kingdom.

QUESTION: Is Misty becoming a new friend?

FRIENDSHIP RULE #3: A true friend introduces you to new and unexpected adventures.

Misty is overjoyed to be reunited with her insect friend. "This is a total cricket miracle!" She throws her

 101

arms around me, which almost causes me to drop the jar on the sidewalk. "My mom is on her way. You've got to keep the jar out of sight. She'll know immediately what's going on if she sees it."

I suggest that I take Sweet Sunshine home overnight and then bring her to school tomorrow. Misty thinks it's a great idea. She can't think of any greater place for hiding out than at the Avatar residence.

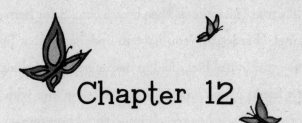

Chapter 12

6:24 P.M.,
PALMVILLE STREET

Indigo and I round the corner to our house, and there is Frederick waiting for us at the bottom of our driveway. As soon as we get out of the car, there's the usual cat-who-thinks-he's a dog routine, lots of tail wagging, frantic panting, and jumping around in crazy circles, going nowhere. When Frederick finally calms down, I show him the extra-large glass soy mayo jar that is now serving as Sweet Sunshine's rent-free condo.

He's curious at first. Then his jealous streak sends all the gray and white fur on his back pointing up to the sky. His sad puppy-dog cat eyes appear to actually fill with tears. I explain, "Sweet Sunshine is just an insect. Besides, she's not mine." Frederick swipes at the jar again with his furry right paw. "It's true," I continue. Then he lets out a Saint Bernard–size growl. "Frederick! You have to understand that Sweet Sunshine was in trouble. I had to rescue her. She belongs to my new friend Misty, who I know will fall in love with you the moment she sets her green-gray-colored eyes on you."

7:13 P.M.,

MY BEDROOM

Dinner is going to be late tonight because of our Mission Impossible cricket rescue. I change into my drawstring pajama pants and my vintage Beatles tee and tune in to my favorite radio station. I take my hat off and balance it on top of the largest book on my book-shelf, *The Absolute Complete Unabridged Version of the History of the World*. That's where I keep the most important piece of evidence about my missing father—a photograph. It's a black-and-white, out-of-focus image that Indigo has confirmed is Patch, my missing father.

IMPORTANT NOTE: Indigo can't remember when she took the photograph but knows for sure that it was before I was born. This photograph still needs more thorough investigation. It's on the must-do-or-else list to solve the Patch case.

I slide the photograph out to take my three-hundred-billionth look at it. I study it carefully, then close my eyes, trying to imagine my father back when he first met Indigo. I'm sure he spoke in a calm, deep voice, and when he laughed, he would send catch-on-fire sound waves across the room. He was most likely perfect in every way.

I then remember that I have to write my punishment essay for Mr. Scuzzy, so I sit at my desk to give it a try. I manage the following short paragraph just as the wind chimes ring from downstairs.

Why I So Entirely Believe in Second Chances
by Portia Avatar

I think second chances are radically cool. Here's why. If you mess up in some ridiculous way, you get to rewind, erase, and do it all over again.

People in general don't get second chances a lot, but when they do, it can change their entire life. On a personal level, I've decided to give new girl a second chance, even though she got me into trouble. Second chances work in really surprising ways. I never would have predicted this latest development. So getting caught red-handed with a note in my hand was actually good luck. Even if it was my first minor offense in the history of attending middle school and now my perfect record is ruined forever. I've learned something new because of the "incident," that maybe people aren't perfect and that's why second chances exist in the first place.

I press save and look up at the ceiling, using my X-ray vision to imagine the night sky just beginning to make its appearance. I silently ask the heavens to please let Mr. Scuzzy accept my essay for what it is, even if it is kind of short. Please let him care more about quality than quantity. Please let him give me a second chance.

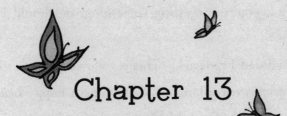

Chapter 13

Dinner Menu at the Avatars
Nearly-a-Burger with Real Cheese
Gluten-Free and Simply Saucy Chili Fries
Crispy Carrot Chips
Over-the-Top Soy Vanilla Yogurt Cups

Crunching on a carrot chip, I eye Indigo suspiciously.

"What's the occasion?"

"You!"

"Me?"

Indigo adds, "And me!" A thunderous growl rumbles

at my feet, which leads Indigo to say, "And Frederick, too! We're all together now. Isn't it wonderful?"

"Mom, you're forgetting something, or should I say someone."

"I included Frederick." This is followed by the sound of Frederick's extra-long tail drumming a happy beat on the floor. Then Indigo adds, "Oh, and of course, our overnight visitor, Sweet Sunshine."

QUESTION: Is Indigo pretending not to know what I'm suggesting?

I look into her deep brown eyes. "Patch! He's still missing, and until he's back home with us sharing a family meal, we're not 'all together.'"

She squirms in her seat. "We're working on it, aren't we?"

"You've been so busy with pomegranates and Rock that there's been 0 percent progress."

Indigo defends herself. "I'm doing my best. I've really been trying, Portia."

"There's no evidence of that, Mom. And now, with

another case on my plate, I don't want to lose ground with our search for Patch."

Gently Indigo reaches for my hand. "Trust me."

I let her hold my hand for exactly three seconds.

Indigo conveniently leaves the table and goes into the kitchen to prepare a mystery dessert, which she pours into a bowl. Then she proudly presents it to me. "Honey-sweetened pomegranate syrup to sample with the vanilla yogurt cups."

IMPORTANT NOTE: It's incredibly obvious that Indigo is using her food skills to avoid any more discussion about the man in our lives who's not in our lives. I can tell she's relieved to be talking about something other than Patch with a capital P.

I quickly slurp up my yogurt covered with sticky red syrup, which actually tastes okay, except for the puckery effect of the pomegranate. Indigo will be happy to hear that I'm giving her tasty dessert 3.75 stars (out of a possible 5). But my food review will have to wait until later because the phone rings, interrupting our evening. It's Rock, one of Palmville's bravest.

To avoid listening in on Indigo and Rock's sticky-sweet conversation, I invite Frederick to join me outside in our backyard garden for some night air. He follows, sniffing madly down the narrow path to one of my all-time favorite spots, the hammock that hangs between two slumping lemon trees. I jump on it, letting my feet touch the sky as I slowly rest my head on the canvas pillow at just the right angle. I've perfected this move over the years, so it's not something I really think about much now. Frederick knows the routine too and follows along, landing squarely on my stomach. It's always the same thing. First I shriek, "Ouch, Frederick! Your paws!" Then he apologizes by licking my face with his rough tongue, begging for forgiveness. Then I say, "I love you, Freddy Fred Frederick!" This evening I add, "You see, here we are having one-on-one time, just like I told you we would!"

Frederick and I swing on the hammock to the tune of the lone bird who lives in one of the trees above us. If I look up through the green leaves huddled together, I can see him singing his evening song. Every once in a while he flaps his wings, showing off the black-and-white-striped pattern Mother Nature has so kindly given him. Maybe his song sounds sweet, but I'm certain that when a bird sings that loudly and that sweetly, it's because he's searching for something, like a girlfriend. So really his sugary melody is kind of a sad song. I look up past the branch at the moon, which only reminds me of Patch, who is somewhere out there living an extraordinarily adventurous life, and who doesn't have a clue that I exist.

IMPORTANT FACT: I've been searching for my father ever since I can remember. I know only a few things about him, mostly from the dreams I have at night, but I have gathered a few vital pieces of evidence, plus some key information.

1. My father's name is Patch.
2. I have a blurry black-and-white photo of him wearing a hat.
3. I've received colorful postcards from him (in my dreams) with super short messages on them, promising an imminent return.
4. I am Patch's daughter.

As I swing back and forth, I realize that the singing feathered bachelor and I have a lot in common. We're both searching for a loved one under the glow of tonight's silvery moon.

A loud giggle travels from the kitchen through the screen door, interrupting the winged Romeo's "where is my true love?" melody. He stops to listen. Then he picks up on Indigo's giggly tune, mixing it with his own, and soon I'm hearing it in stereo.

> **FACT:** Indigo and Rock's hide-and-seek relationship weighs on my mind. Rock is not my father and can never own the piece of my heart designated for fathers. I could never imagine a substitute father living under the same roof.

I swing back and forth, staring at the moon, plugging my ears from the chirping, singing, giggling bird above me and from Indigo's extra loud and extra long conversation with Rock. I decide to take out my PDA to see what digital news has come my way.

There are two messages waiting for me. The first one is marked "Extremely Urgent," and it's from Mademoiselle Clamdigger.

To: pavatar@palmville.net

From: mememe@palmville.net

Why are you still hanging out with freaky girl?
Do you have any idea how many international
germs insects carry? :O! Ame

P.S. What are you wearing tomorrow?

P.P.S. I'll see you at Purple Haze after school, *oui*?

IMPORTANT QUESTION: Why does Amy con-
tinue to be so concerned about me spending time with Misty?
Doesn't she know that I'm her best friend and nothing is ever
going to change that?

I quickly reply to her message to reassure her that our
friendship is still on solid ground.

To: mememe@palmville.net

From: pavatar@palmville.net

 113

I've got the perfect hat for the new case! I can't wait to show it to you. I think you're going to love it as much as I do! Yes, I'll be there at Purple Haze for the shopping date. I love that place! You know that you can always count on me, Amy. Your true friend, Portia

I read the second message. It's from Misty.

To: pavatar@palmville.net
From: animalsrule@palmville.net

How's my Sweet Sunshine? If she's with the Avatars, I have no doubt she's doing amazingly well. But Maxwell is a different story completely. I've been observing him for hours now. His behavior has gone from really strange to really, truly strange. He's hissing like a cat every time I come near him now, and he still won't eat. And he's even bigger than he was yesterday! You have to see this for yourself. Do you have time to stop by after school tomorrow? Your biggest fan, Misty.

P.S. You are positively the coolest friend ever! :-D

To: animalsrule@palmville.net
From: pavatar@palmville.net

Continue observing the subject. His behavior is truly mystifying. Let's talk in the a.m. about a visit to the canyons. Not sure I'll be able to make it. BTW, Sweet Sunshine seems to be enjoying herself. Indigo is feeding her a variety of homegrown treats, so no worries in the raw food department. C U tomorrow, P :)

BIG PROBLEM: Both Misty and Amy want to meet me at the same time tomorrow for two different reasons!

FACT: I can't be in two places at once.

Indigo is finally off the phone. She waves at me through the screen door. With dueling friends, one new and one old, occupying my mind, I make my nightly trek to my bedroom. Indigo interrupts my train of thought, gently grabbing my hand. "You're right, Portia, we've got to change the direction of the search. It's time for a new approach." Her voice crescendos with renewed energy. "Let's reserve Sunday nights for a Patch Powwow, where we gather all our research and findings from each week. That way we'll always be on the same page, and we'll be able to compare notes about our progress. Sound good?"

I give my mom a giant polar bear hug, which we both know means, Yes, that is so entirely cool of you to step up the search!

Chapter 14

A morning phone call from Rock interferes with Indigo's latest breakfast creation. She's attempting pomegranate waffles with wild cherry and lime organic spread. My taste buds beg for something simple. Perhaps a bowl of Corn Flakes? But her insistent look demands I taste her pomegranate creation. I twist my fork into her newly imagined red-tinted breakfast, while she heads to the refrigerator and takes out my prepared lunch, meticulously packed in a reusable lunch bag. She balances the phone under one ear and hands me my packed lunch, all while dancing to an invisible beat.

QUESTION: What does Mr. Hero say to my mother that sends her in such an embarrassing direction back in time to when she was in high school and had football-star crushes?

Indigo finally hangs up from her conversation with the firefighter. She adjusts her long single braid, then pulls a stool up to the table. "I must hear about last night's dreams. I've been waiting all morning!"

"That's impossible, Indigo. You've been on the phone all morning."

"Just one dream will do, Portia."

"Nothing comes to me."

FACT: My mother is a professional Dream Checker. She's an expert at interpreting symbols and finding below-the-surface meaning in things like elephants, waterfalls, and golden butterflies. Mornings are usually the times she enjoys perfecting her skillful interpretations.

Frederick interrupts his morning leftover pomegranate waffle to chase my PDA (which has mysteriously found its way to the kitchen floor), swatting at it like it's some sort of giant bug. When I finally retrieve it, I see that I have a message from Misty. She's super psyched that Sweet Sunshine is "coming home" today. She instructs me to meet her at the front entrance of school and promises that she'll be prompt!

Indigo gathers her necessities for another busy day at The Tent. She juggles freshly picked limes and lemons from our backyard, then packs them into her "Green Is My Favorite Color" hemp bag. She tosses a small piece of lettuce into the soy mayo jar presently housing Sweet Sunshine, providing the three-legged insect with some morning nourishment. "We'll get back to your dreams later, Portia. I expect a full report."

Trying to make my mother happy, at least until she discovers that there are in fact no dreams to report, I respond, "Okay, Mom."

7:47 A.M.,
PALMVILLE STREET

J hold the jar containing Sweet Sunshine on my lap. My knapsack rests precariously on the car floor in front of me. Our hybrid quietly heads toward town. I watch Frederick sitting at the edge of the driveway, staring at our car. I stare back at him, even though he can't see me.

At the first red light, Indigo glances down at Sweet Sunshine, who is happily chewing on her piece of fresh homegrown lettuce. "We make quite a team, don't we?"

"Yes. That was an inspiring rescue last night!"

"I was wondering how the case with Misty is progressing. Has the Sweet Sunshine rescue provided you with any new insights?"

"It's confidential, Mom. Anything I've told you about the case, and what's happened between you, me, and Sweet Sunshine, is entirely classified."

With a smile on her face, she calmly says, "You can count on me. I won't reveal anything to anyone at any time, now or in the future." She stops the car at the front entrance of Palmville Middle School and sneaks a kiss on my cheek. "Have a beautiful day at school."

I place Sweet Sunshine securely on the passenger seat while I grab my knapsack and step out to greet the world of middle school once again. Indigo zooms off, but then I see her put on the brakes and carefully back up. Through the opened window, she hands me Sweet Sunshine. "I think you forgot something. Or should I say, someone."

"Thanks, Mom. Good luck with the pomegranates." This time she zooms off and keeps going all the way to The Tent to start her long day of inventing recipes and baking, roasting, and grilling vegetarian, preservative-free delights.

8:01 A.M., THE FRONT STEPS, PALMVILLE MIDDLE SCHOOL

I prep for the much rumored math quiz while waiting for Misty, who seems to be late a lot. I quickly make a note of this fact and then get back to math madness. As I search for the chapter that I'm certain we'll be tested on, the postcards that Vera had given Misty fall to the bottom concrete step just below me. I lean forward to gather all three of them, quickly glancing at the short messages on each card. The words send my imagination spinning back in time to when they were written. For fun, I try to picture the people who wrote them.

POSTCARD #1:

A FADED IMAGE OF
A BOUQUET OF INTERWEAVING VIOLETS.

Valentine . . .
Please rush to me now. For our
lives are destined to be together.
Forever yours,
Willie

Willie was surely young and in love. Maybe he was on leave from a World War.

POSTCARD #2:

A PHOTO OF MOUNT RUSHMORE
WITH A SCRIPTED MESSAGE,
"FACES OF THE FABULOUS FOUR."

Dear Aunt Sylvia,
Just a line to let you know that we got this
far without any trouble, not even a flat!
Love from Etienne, Joseph, and Rose

The third postcard strikes me as different from the others. It doesn't appear to be as old-fashioned. The image invites me to wonder where it is and why its writer has traveled so far away from home. I've never seen an ocean so crystal blue. The sandy beach, in contrast, is a pure white. Tall green ferns sway in the breeze. There's not a person, animal, or building in sight. It's a desert island! What sparks my curiosity most about this image is the message printed in a bright, sunshine yellow color on the upper right corner. It reads, "Imagine."

I turn over the card with great anticipation. Whispering the message to myself, I read the note.

Aloha, Vera.
Your glorious gift is beyond description.
Fondly, Patch

My whole body shakes as I spell out the letters. P-A-T-C-H. It's him! This is a postcard from my nowhere-to-be-found father!

All I see is the postcard. Everything else around me is a total blur. My heart beats faster as I check the address, and there it is, Trash and Treasures, 278 Main Street, Palmville, CA. That means Vera knew Patch! They even had a correspondence!

IMPORTANT QUESTIONS: Why would Vera pretend not to know my father? Why would she let me run around in circles trying to find him when she clearly possesses key information about him?

IMPORTANT FACT: No real friend would do that to another friend.

I feel a tap on my shoulder, which shakes me from the mild state of shock in which I find myself. I look up, and it's Webster. "Ms. Avatar."

I gasp. "Webster! It wasn't supposed to be you!"

"Are you certain about that?"

"Yes, absolutely!"

He scratches his head. "I was wondering something."

"Oh?"

"It's a personal question. Do you mind?"

I look around for Misty to appear and rescue me

from this really uncomfortable boy/girl exchange. "Is it the same question you were going to ask me a few days ago?"

"Uh, I was wondering . . ."

The first bell rings, signaling that we have two minutes to get to Mr. Scuzzy's class. I grab my knapsack and stand up so quickly that I lose my grip on Sweet Sunshine's glass home. Webster tries to help me prevent the jar from hitting the ground and shattering into a thousand pieces. As we struggle to keep the jar from falling, the cover loosens and out jumps a very anxious Sweet Sunshine.

She immediately crawls around the back of my shirt! With a book bag on my back and a glass jar now in my right hand, I take my left hand and try desperately to catch Sweet Sunshine, causing my books to spill from the bag, flying into the air. Webster leaps to the rescue, carefully collecting the books one at a time for me.

I spot Sweet Sunshine crawling down my sleeve now. "Sweet Sunshine, you're still with me. Please remain calm. I've got you!" I delicately catch the orphaned cricket and place her inside the jar. Webster stands there, witnessing my goofy cricket dance. He's got my books piled neatly on the steps. And he's retrieved the postcard from Patch, my new groundbreaking piece of material evidence for the case.

I am so overjoyed to have rescued Sweet Sunshine for the second time in twenty-four hours that my hands spring forward, grabbing Webster and giving him a major-motion-picture hug. He backs away with an "I've just seen a ghost" expression on his face, stumbling down the path to the main entrance of school. I look down at my shoes, and there, under my left foot, is the essay I wrote for Mr. Scuzzy on second chances. It's torn down the center, with Webster's footprints on it, and now it's got mine on it too.

W.H. and I are bonded together through our footprints on my punishment essay. I make a quick mental note of this potentially poignant fact, then race the second bell before I start accumulating even more middle school demerits.

As I rush to class I smile, knowing that I have concrete evidence of my father's existence tucked inside my back pocket. Vera was right. Nothing ever stays the same.

Chapter 15

Misty has been trying to get my attention ever since she walked in late to Scuzzy's class. I've got Sweet Sunshine safely nestled between my hat and my math textbook, which are all buried deep inside my book bag. I refuse to even acknowledge Misty. If I do, I might receive an even worse punishment than writing an essay, since third chances are rarely, if ever, granted by teachers.

Every time Scuzzy turns around to write on the board, Misty loud-whispers to me, "Is she here? Do you really have her in your very own possession? I can't believe you found her!" She grins so wide I think her mouth will break. Her braces sparkle in the morning sun. I look at her only from the corner of my eye. Besides the fact that her purple-tinted braces look extra bright this morning, I notice that she's got a monster pink Band-Aid on her left arm. The plastic strip seems to be hiding red scratch marks.

Mr. Scuzzy is staring at me, repeating my name slowly. "Portia?"

"Hi!"

"Hello, Portia. Now can you tell us how you view twenty-first-century media as it relates to your life."

"Isn't that kind of personal?"

Mr. S. thinks seriously about what I've just asked. "Interesting. What you're saying is that with the Internet and cell phones and PDAs, media has become personal."

Following along, I'm surprised how easily I dug my way out of this potentially disastrous teacher/student moment. "Absolutely."

Then Mr. S. has an idea. "I'd love to hear more about your theory. How about gifting us with a short essay on it for class tomorrow?"

I smile and agree to the assignment. Do I really have a choice?

QUESTION: Why is Mr. S. so essay-crazy?

I mentally take note of Mr. Scuzzy's possible personality problem. Then it hits me that he said "tomorrow." That means the day after today! This mystifying case starring Misty Longfellow is turning out to have a not-so-kind impact on my free time.

Class sludges forward until the bell finally rings. That's when Misty races over to me. "So extraordinarily sorry I was late today!" She waves her bandaged arm in my face. "Maxwell was extra moody this morning." She looks around for the soy mayo jar. "Where is she? I've got to see my little girl!"

I lead Misty to my locker, then slowly take Sweet Sunshine's glass condo out of my book bag and hand it to her. She's so overjoyed that she does an ancient rain dance in the middle of the hall. Her dance is so jungle-crazy that she loses her grip on Sweet Sunshine's temporary home and sends the glass jar flying high into the air. I reach out with both hands to catch it. But another set of hands is there first, intercepting and catching it just before it comes crashing down to the floor.

The two hands and ten fingers belong to Webster!

Misty is horrified at what's she's almost done. When Webster calmly hands her the jar, she quickly checks out Sweet Sunshine, who is shaken, but not stirred. She stares at Sweet Sunshine's big bug eyes. "I promise never to forget you, my Sunshine." She turns to Webster, but it's no surprise that he's already off to earth science class to challenge his brain cells.

IMPORTANT NOTE: Webster is revealing a whole new side of himself with this second heroic act of total self-sacrifice for a cricket.

Then I remember something important. Webster and I held hands and hugged in less than one week!

SECRET TRUTH: Even though Amy insists that my maybe crush on Webster Holiday is fictional, I'm starting to think it might be real.

The bell for my next class is about to ring. I hand Misty the postcards Vera gave her, except for the one safe inside my back pocket. "Is it okay if I keep one? There's something about it that reminds me of someone very important to me."

Happy and grateful for me rescuing Sweet Sunshine and for trying to figure out Maxwell's ongoing psychological problem, Misty enthusiastically says, "Of course!" Then she adds, "So, you'll be coming by to see Maxwell, right?"

"I've got a very busy afternoon."

Misty discloses alarming new details about the subject. "Maxwell has gone through a complete and total personality change. Now he's snapping, growling, scratching, and snarling!"

I don't want to break my date with Amy, and I've got to go to Trash and Treasures and The Tent to investigate the new material evidence for the Patch case in the form of a postcard, so I suggest, "What if I come by later in the day?"

Misty's voice cracks with emotion. "I've never had a friend . . . like you before!"

The bell rings and I scramble to my next class, managing to leap into my seat with a forced smile on my face just before the bell has finished its tinny, shrilly ring. A star is born when I casually reach for my social studies notebook as if life right now were totally normal.

2:35 P.M., MATH CLASS, PALMVILLE MIDDLE SCHOOL

I've spent every free minute of the day sneaking peeks at practice quizzes and printed worksheets. Now it's quiz time! When Miss Killjoy hands me the long-awaited math test, which has been pestering me like a hungry mosquito, I surprise myself. I calmly thank her and slowly, with confidence, complete the test before every other kid in the class, with the exception of Webster Holiday, of course.

FACT: My current state of calm has to do with my discovery this morning. Once the radical shock of reading the postcard wore off, I found myself floating on a cloud. I'm still riding on it.

Without being too obvious about it, I slip this extraordinary piece of my family puzzle out of my pocket to look at it again. It's real! Then I quickly slip it back inside my pocket for safekeeping.

It's five minutes before class ends, so I decide to review the quiz one more time. This time I notice I missed a question. It's for bonus points too.

Bonus Question: Does Math Matter?

Since I'm the newly anointed queen of essays, I decide to give it a try. Here's my answer:

At first I wondered the same thing. Does math matter? But recently I stumbled on what can only be described as a miracle. The odds of me finding this certain object, which cannot be disclosed because its content is personal in nature (and has nothing to do with math), are nearly impossible, and yet it happened. The only way I can explain it is probability, statistics, and chance all wrapped up in one of the best presents I could ever ask for. As I think about it now, math can explain a lot of seemingly inexplicable events in life, even how the universe works and why there are so many stars in the sky. So, does math matter? Yes! It matters to me a lot.

A collective sigh is heard in class when the bell rings. The highly anticipated Killjoy pop quiz is now officially over.

Chapter 16

Amy drops her sketch pad accidentally on purpose directly in front of my locker. Dipping down, she casually flips through the pages filled with colorful drawings. "Pardon *moi*, is this mine?"

"You've got more sketches. I must see what you've been up to at once!"

With a devilish grin, Amy insists, "I'm saving them for later, when we get together. We are meeting up at Purple Haze, aren't we?"

"You're not going to believe what happened. I stumbled on a postcard with Patch's name on it. Actually,

Misty found it when we were at Trash and Treasures. It's a huge, potentially earth-shattering breakthrough in the Patch case."

Eyeing my newly discovered plaid detective hat, Amy asks, "Where did you pick that up?"

"It's the new hat I wrote you about. Misty found it!"

"Of course she did. So what time are we going to meet?"

"Amy, this afternoon is so jammed. I've got to investigate why Vera has never revealed to me that she knew Patch, and then I have to track down Indigo to discuss this new piece of incredible evidence."

Amy dramatically slides the sketchbook into one of her dozen designer school totes that she alternates every day of the week.

I continue, "And Misty's bunny is seriously freaking out! He needs me!"

Amy smacks her lips together. "So glad you and new girl are becoming such good friends."

"What a relief. I thought it was bothering you. Hey, I've got a great idea. Let's all hang out tomorrow!"

"I don't think so. I've got this new friend, and . . ."

Amy checks her pink bubblegum watch. "Look at the time. I really must go!"

IMPORTANT FACT: My attempt at finding a way to bring an old friend and a new friend together has clearly backfired. Amy has zero interest in spending time with Misty.

3:23 P.M.,

TRASH AND TREASURES

This afternoon Vera wears a straw cowgirl hat, a white T-shirt, and a pair of cut-off jean shorts that cover her knees. She's polishing an over-the-top set of silverware from an era I haven't studied yet in school. She lifts a decorative salad fork against the hanging factory light and casually asks, without looking at me, "How's the case?"

I respond, "Which one?"

She turns to me. "Take your pick!"

I spring into action. In 100 percent investigation mode, I begin, "How long have you lived in Palmville?"

"Since I was born. I've never lived anywhere else."

"Interesting."

Setting the fork on the counter, Vera asks, "Something to share?"

"I found new evidence today, by accident."

Vera then leans against the table, searching for the answer in my eyes. "Now you've got my full attention. Spill."

Checking to see if my hat is still on my head (it is!), I confront Vera. "You knew my father, didn't you?"

Without missing even half a beat, she answers, "Yes, I did."

I slip out the postcard signed by Patch and hand it to her. "I thought you were my friend!"

She smiles knowingly. Then, with a mellow tone in her voice, she tells me, "Everything has its own timing."

I don't say a word, but my face says everything. Vera knows that she owes me more than a cloudy day explanation. She continues with her side of the story. "It just hasn't been the right time to reveal what I know yet."

QUESTIONS: What is Vera not telling me and why?

I take charge of the moment. "I have an idea. Come to the Patch Powwow on Sunday. Indigo and I are going to review the case. I think you might be of some help."

Vera is middle-of-the-night quiet. I count to twelve. Then she finally responds, "Is there a time I should show up at your doorstep?"

Careful not to let any hint of emotion slip out, I say, "Dinner will be served at seven."

With a smile and a wink, Vera says, "Sunday at seven it shall be."

To avoid any more awkwardness between me and my "friend" Vera, I use the "I have so much homework" excuse to slip out of Trash and Treasures and make my way to The Tent to tell Indigo the news of my radical finding and to ponder this unexpected twist in the case of my missing father.

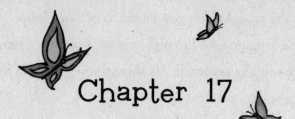

Chapter 17

I slip through The Tent's back door, reserved for employees, delivery people, and me, calling out for Indigo, "Mom, are you here? I need to talk to you!"

Indigo is in her office, balancing her phone against her shoulder while lighting a soy pear candle on her desk. She quickly shakes out the match. "Oh no! Call me later!"

I try to piece together the other part of this dramatic exchange. Indigo calms herself with a deep yoga breath before reaching out both arms for a hug. I oblige, but I can tell that she's still thinking about her most recent telephone conversation. I ask, "Who was that?"

"Rock. The wind has taken a dangerous turn, and he's been stuck up in the canyons since last night!"

"Sorry to hear that."

Indigo's nervous eyes insist that I switch lanes, so I do. "I read something today that's going to change my life and yours forever."

"A book?"

"Not a book."

Indigo leans a little closer to me. I show her the card that I've been concealing in my back pocket. "It's a post-card from Patch!"

Indigo turns so pale that she matches the newly painted office wall. I hand her the card. Her hands tremble as she studies the image and then turns it over to read the message. She quietly asks, "Where did you get this?"

"Misty found it at Trash and Treasures."

Her eyes fill with tears. "This isn't the right time."

"When is the right time?"

She hands me back the card. "Let's hold off on this until Sunday."

I take the card and slip it back into my pocket. "Vera

will be joining us too. She's got a lot to share, and my guess is that she'll offer important new evidence for the case."

Indigo remains perfectly still. "I thought this was going to be an evening reserved for just the two of us."

"The case is bigger than us now. We need Vera. She knew Patch. Why didn't you tell me that crucial bit of information?"

Hap rushes up to the door, interrupting this tension-filled conversation. "The pomegranate cake is ready!"

Indigo looks over at him, preoccupied with thoughts of Patch and my new discovery. "I'll be right there."

He's convinced that he said something wrong. "So terribly sorry," he says, backing out of the room. "I'll be in the kitchen."

Walking on eggshells, avoiding a late afternoon argument, Indigo turns to me. "I've got to get back to work."

I check my watch and see it's getting late. I still have to get over to Misty's house to check on Maxwell. "I've got to go now too. The mystifying Misty case is heating up."

Indigo tries to ease the tension in the room by redirecting the conversation. "How are things going?"

Tilting my head to one side to get my point across, I tell her, "It's top secret."

"I understand, sweetheart."

"Thanks for accepting my double life."

Her face relaxes. "Of course, honey. Just be back in time for dinner."

I assure her that I will.

Then I step out into the dining room and wave goodbye to Hap, who is closely examining a pomegranate. Indigo calls out to me, "Portia, why don't you bring Misty a piece of the pomegranate cake? I have a feeling she could use something sweet today."

Hap senses an opportunity. Losing his grip on the kooky fruit, he stutters, "I'll get right on it, Indigo!" When he says the word "Indigo," it sounds like it's a sacred artifact to be worshipped and admired. He scrambles behind the counter, quickly packaging a piece of pomegranate cake for me to take to Misty.

I'm just about out the door when Indigo calls, "There's been a change of plans."

"Okay."

"Rock will be joining us for dinner tonight. That's assuming he can get off his shift on time."

Upon overhearing this bit of unfortunate news, Hap drops a drinking glass on the floor; it shatters everywhere.

I shout back, "I wasn't thinking about that kind of change of plans."

Indigo states her case. "Rock has been fighting fires for two weeks straight. He needs a home-cooked meal. Hurry along, your case is waiting."

4:57 P.M.,

PALMVILLE'S DUSTY CANYONS

Three fire trucks pass by me in less than five minutes. I'm almost up the hill to Misty's house, but first I have to walk by Webster's abode. As I do, I casually sneak a peek at the front yard, which is surrounded by tall green pines. My eyes must be doing tricks on me, because what I see is too unbelievable to actually be nonfiction.

 144

It's Webster and Amy sitting on a blanket together, reading a book. I rub my eyes extra hard and take a second look. Amy catches my eye. She waves emphatically at me, wearing a sly smile.

QUESTION: Could Webster be the "new friend" that Amy has been referring to all week?

I decide to run as fast as I can up to Misty's house.

QUESTIONS: I wonder if Amy set up the date with Webster to get back at me for canceling our shopping spree at Purple Haze. I wonder if Amy C. is actually jealous of my new friendship with Misty L. Could Amy and Webster truly be "seeing" each other?

MINUTES LATER,
MISTY'S BACKYARD

When I get to Misty's house, I race over to her, out of breath, and tell her, "I'm thrilled to be here!"

Misty doesn't know how to react to this sudden show of friendship. Her only response is to do four cartwheels in a row.

IMPORTANT NOTE: Misty seems to really care about me and completely and totally appreciate me. She's certainly not someone who would ever think about stealing my secret crush, like an unnamed person down the hill whose initials are A.C.

Maxwell is napping, so my consultation is temporarily delayed. To pass the time, I sit on Misty's drought-resistant lawn, watching her perform an endless series of cartwheels. She finally takes a break. That's when I offer her the piece of Indigo's pomegranate cake. She opens the package slowly, savoring the moment like it's Christmas morning. When she sees that it's a piece of cake, she's even more enthusiastic. She samples a generous portion. "This is amazing! Your mom is so super amazing! I want to thank her personally for baking this delectable treat. It's simply scrumptious!" She proceeds to attempt a forward flip, which she misses completely, landing right on her derriere.

I run over to her. "Misty, are you okay?"

She laughs uncontrollably. Then we both hear Maxwell let out a loud squeal from under his fleece tent. He's awakened from his nap! Misty immediately switches to a serious mood. "There's no time to waste. You've got to talk to Maxwell."

Maxwell's shelter is in shambles. The blanket is full of tiny tears. Sharp little teeth marks have bitten into everything in a five-foot radius. It's a full-on demolition derby. And there is Maxwell, madly chewing on an old sock in fast motion, with his eyes stuck in a cold stare.

Misty throws up her long, skinny arms. "Please help, Detective Avatar!"

I immediately adjust my newsboy hat, then tiptoe forward. This startles poor Maxwell, who changes position slightly and returns to his frozen state. Then he stares at me for two long seconds, darts away, and disappears into the darkest and most hidden corner of his hideaway.

Misty's big hazel eyes well up with tears. We hear a car pulling into the driveway. It's Misty's mom! Misty dries her tears with her jaguar-inspired cardigan. "My mom cannot know this is happening! We must make up a story. Hurry! Why are you here?"

Mrs. Longfellow breezes by us with barely a wave. Misty breathes a sigh of relief, that is, until Mrs. L. turns around and backtracks to us. We start pretending we're gossiping about boys. In a loud voice, I giggle, "That Webster sure is cute!"

Misty forgets that she's acting. "Really? I've been wondering about you two."

I stretch my eyes as wide as they will go, trying to remind Misty that we're creating an improvisational fiction here!

Mrs. L. takes the bait, looking first at me and then at Misty. "Misty, you're with your new friend again."

"Mother, she's not just my new friend. She's my best friend!"

I play along and chime in, "It's true!"

Misty forgets that she's acting again. "Really truly, Portia?"

I smile through my teeth. "Of course. I mean, I've known you less than a school week, but it's like we're sisters separated at birth."

Misty is overwhelmed. "I can't believe my ears! This is—"

Mrs. L. interrupts Misty's joyride. "—all so wonderful, Mysteria. You finally found a friend. Now you won't be wasting your time with those creatures of yours. Hurry along. There must be homework you have to do this afternoon."

Misty suddenly calls upon her inner acclaimed actress. "Of course, Mother. Portia was just leaving. I'll be right there."

As soon as Mrs. L. steps into the house, Misty looks into my eyes, and I do the same to her. We both break out giggling at the same time. We're so loud that Maxwell comes out of his hiding place to see what the noise is all about. I catch my breath finally, then the gigglefest begins all over again.

QUESTION: I wonder if friends just sneak up on you just when you're looking the other way.

With the exception of playing a leading role in introducing me to my first detention and the fine art of essay writing, Misty is bringing a lot of interesting adventures into my life. She is definitely unique.

FRIENDSHIP RULE #4: True friends come in all shapes, sizes, and colors.

Now that Maxwell has revealed himself, I quickly check him out to see if I can determine why he is behaving so oddly. I pull out all the tricks I perform for Frederick to get him to eat, but nothing works, not even the Guess What Hand the Cat Food Is In? which is always the clincher. I'm stumped. I make a note of his actions and Misty's reactions, then wave good-bye as I head down the winding road toward home for dinner with Indigo, Frederick, and our special guest.

Chapter 18

Frederick's tail wags left to right. He's slurping up all the attention he's getting from me after a long day of playing alone. Then he stops short and just stares at me. He sniffs me up and down like an investigator on prime-time television. He wisely suspects that I've been spending time with another animal again, but he still hasn't figured out if it's a cat or not, so he keeps sniffing. I pet the white fur puddle shape on the back of his neck. "Have no fear. I would never substitute you for another four-legged creature." He rolls over and plays dead. I playfully sneak up behind him to rub his speckled belly, but he quickly darts out the door and down the stairs.

My PDA sounds off to a new tune. It's Misty. Without even saying hello, I ask, "How's Maxwell?"

She whispers, "He's not responding to anything."

The wind chimes ring. I rush Misty off the phone. "Dinner is on the table. I'll text you later."

Misty whispers again, "Enjoy your home-cooked meal. I'll keep watch over Maxwell . . . Portia."

The chimes ring a second time, even louder this time. "I've really got to go."

Misty adds, "I'm so glad you're the detective on this case. I know that Maxwell's situation is perplexing and taking a lot of your free time, but there's got to be a breakthrough soon. I just know it. I still can't believe you're actually helping me — I mean, helping Maxwell."

"I'll text you later." I hang up. But before heading downstairs, I quickly update my latest findings.

LATEST DEVELOPMENTS ON THE MYSTIFYING MISTY CASE: Misty is still crazy about her rescued helpless creatures, but she appears to be relaxing into the idea of having a human friend.

FACT: I'm actually starting to have fun with this new girl.

NEXT LINE OF ACTION: Determine why Misty still trusts her instincts more with animals than with people.

I hear Indigo giggling at high volume from downstairs. There's a deep voice that's laughing along with her. I can only deduce that the voice belongs to Rock. He's here!

QUESTION: Why do firefighters have a habit of arriving on time or even early? Is that part of their special training?

I find my seat at the table, only to discover that Rock has already claimed it. There are Avatar family rules, and Rock has just broken a major one!

FACT: Each family member has a designated spot at the dining room table. Every evening I slip onto my antique wooden chair. Frederick weaves between my feet below me until he finds his favorite spot under the table. Indigo's seat is opposite mine. She misses out on enjoying the backyard garden view. Instead she faces the kitchen, usually with an eye on the next course

153

bubbling on the stove or roasting in the oven. And then there's the chair at the head of the table that I have secretly reserved for Patch. No one ever sits there!

Tonight this important family ritual is shaken by a happy-go-lucky heroic type, whose endless stories of rescue and sacrifice are sure to smother any possibility of decent dinner conversation.

As politely as I can, I begin tonight's official dinner-time chat. "Hi, Rock. That's my seat."

Rock stands up, slowly imitating a cowboy. "Pardon me, Miss Portia," he says, tipping an invisible hat. Then he casually sidles over to Patch's chair and makes himself comfortable there. I feel a tinge of upper back pain as soon he pulls in the chair and makes his new position official. My neck twitches as he shouts over to Indigo, "Whatever you're cooking, I put in a request in advance for seconds."

In my imagination, I roll my eyes, but in the real world, I fake a smile.

QUESTION: Why are grown-ups so obvious about 99.5 percent of everything?

Trying to recreate our family dinner ritual even though Rock is in the process of invading our nearly perfect existence, I call out to my gray and white best friend, "Frederick. It's dinner!"

Galloping into the dining room, Frederick passes me by, excitedly jumping onto Rock's lap instead. He purrs loudly, showering him with a dozen wet kitty cat kisses.

QUESTION: Is Frederick's obvious betrayal a way to get back at me for not giving him enough attention this past week? Or could it be that he actually likes Rock and wants to sit on his lap?

Rock takes full advantage of the situation. "I don't know what it is about me, but animals love me. I once rescued a cat and . . ." He begins to rattle on about yet another heroic deed.

I cover my mouth, letting out a big yawn.

Indigo immediately deflects my conspicuous behavior. "Long day today?"

Rock jumps in. "It's been tough out there. And there's still no letup in sight."

Indigo turns to me and asks, "How about you, Portia? Did you make any progress at Misty's?"

With an exaggerated arm stretch, I yawn again. "I collected a lot of crucial data, and I'm exhausted. I hope I'll be able to make it through dinner."

Indigo looks at me, but I know she's really talking to Rock. "Why don't you start with the pomegranate yogurt dip and rice chips?"

With a full mouth, Rock crunches, "Did you make these chips yourself?"

Indigo answers demurely, "I did."

I look at Frederick for a little support. He can't possibly be enjoying this little one-act play that is unfolding before our eyes. But he's still purring up a storm, brushing up against Rock's muscular arms now.

Before I can suggest that "since it's been such a long day, I think it's best that I have my dinner upstairs so I can finish all my homework," the doorbell rings.

NOTE: At our house, the doorbell ring is not your typical *ding-dong* kind of ring. It's more of a sequence of choreographed bells you might hear if you're traveling over the Himalayas on your way to a Tibetan wedding.

Indigo excuses herself from the table and takes long, graceful strides to the front door. I can barely hear her feet hit the ground. I lean over my chair to see who's there. It's Hap, balancing two giant bags of pomegranates and stumbling down the hall. Forget homework! Now this little soap opera is getting interesting. I wait with anticipation to see what's going to happen next between the lovesick Hap and the mighty Rock.

Indigo leads Hap into the kitchen. He's taking his time, relishing the golden moment that he has just stolen from Indigo. I wave to him.

Rock bellows, "What did the delivery boy bring?" Frederick jumps off Rock's lap and immediately circles Hap, hissing at him, while every few seconds swiping at his calves. Hap tries to appeal to Frederick's adorable cat-ness but fails miserably.

FACT: Cats have strong and definite opinions of people.

Rock calmly calls Frederick over to him. Frederick then retreats from his surprise attack on Hap and jumps back onto Rock's lap, purring at an exceptionally high volume now.

It's intermission, so I excuse myself from the table. "Indigo, I'll just grab a plate of whatever and do my homework upstairs."

Indigo can't exactly argue with her daughter, who dutifully offers to do her homework, but she tries to convince me to stay anyway. "Are you sure you don't want to join us?"

I present a totally legitimate excuse. "I've got an essay to write. I really should get to it."

With a big sigh, Indigo prepares a plate of grilled tofu and other healthy surprises for me. Hap waits patiently, still clutching his two bags of pomegranates, trying to figure out where to place them in the kitchen without getting in Indigo's way. He also tries hard not to respond to Rock's "joke" about him being a delivery boy. But he can no longer suppress his male pride and finally blurts out, "I'm an assistant chef!"

I quickly slip away upstairs, happy to avoid any more of this embarrassing display of random grown-up theatrics.

I take exactly one bite of the grilled tofu and two and half bites of the apple pomegranate relish and sweet potatoes on my plate. Then I grab my PDA to see what messages have arrived in my virtual mailbox. There's a message from Misty.

To: pavatar@palmville.net
From: animalsrule@palmville.net

Portia, would you please tell Indigo thank
you for the tasty cake? Also, I'd appreciate
a call when you've completed your most
perfect dinner with your so-cool-I-practically-
can't-believe-she's-your-mother Indigo.
The fact is that Maxwell is still the absolute
saddest bunny in the physical known
universe.
BFF, Misty

I press Misty's preprogrammed cell number on my PDA. She picks up after one ring. "It's you!"

"It's me. I can't talk long. I've got Scuzzy's essay to write on media and me."

"You can do it. You can do anything, Portia."

"Thanks. I'd better go. It's getting late."

"Wait! Before you hang up, I have a question."

"Okay."

"How was dinner?"

"Since you asked, I witnessed my mother acting like a twelfth grader flirting with tonight's special guest, Rock, the friendly firefighter. Then I watched as she ignored her super cool assistant chef, who showed up all teary-eyed. He blessed her with two bags of pomegranates but then got totally insulted by the firefighter-dude for his efforts."

"Your family sounds incredible! I don't want to be too pushy, but I'd love to see the whole Avatar family experience in live action one day soon. Hey! I just decided where I want to live someday! Your house!"

"But you've got a great canyon hideaway."

"Nobody is ever home. My brother is at boarding school and my parents work all the time. All my mom

 160

cares about is if I did my homework or not, and of course if I've adopted a new animal. My family seriously fails to comprehend me."

"But you're so easy to comprehend. You love animals and you totally appreciate your friends."

"Gosh, that's the nicest thing anyone has ever said to me."

Just then Amy sends an emergency text message. I'd better see what she has to say. I sign off with Misty. "Oh no! I've got an incoming emergency message."

Misty insists, "One more question. Can we have lunch together tomorrow?"

"Sure. Good night, Misty."

Just as I hang up, my PDA flashes again.

To: pavatar@palmville.net
From: mememe@palmville.net

P., what are you wearing tomorrow? This is vitally important, because we mustn't clash when we sit together at lunch. I've decided to forgive you for everything. And you're going

to flip out when you see what I've come up
with for your sweet new detective outfit.
Magic and rainbows, Amy

QUESTION: Is this Amy's way of apologizing to me?

I immediately text her back.

To: mememe@palmville.net
From: pavatar@palmville.net

I've got lunch plans with Misty tomorrow. Do
you want to join us? Bye! Portia

Amy responds before I can count to twenty.

To: pavatar@palmville.net
From: mememe@palmville.net

I read on the Internet that fleabites can
definitely lead to the bubonic plague. You
haven't been hanging around any furry

 162

creatures lately, have you? Oh dear, I've got a
message from W.H., my new best friend! I
guess you figured that out already. Really
must absolutely sign off now. Please don't
count on me joining you for lunch. I might be
busy. Please say hi to Misty for me. Gummy
bears and tulips, Amy

I am officially losing my patience with Amy's covert
behavior.

QUESTIONS: Why can't Amy just tell me what's on
her mind? What do I have to guess the inner meaning of Amy
Clamdigger's text messages?

SPECIAL NOTE: Amy's cloak-and-dagger friendship
makes me think that someday she will be the subject of one of
my future cases.

AN HOUR LATER,
MY BEDROOM

Twenty-First-Century
Media and Technology . . . and Me
by Portia Avatar

Friendships are built and broken through twenty-first-century media and technology. If I didn't have my trusty PDA with me at all times, I wouldn't know half of what I do about my friends. We share so much when the airwaves are clear and our digital signals aren't crossed. At the moment, I'm learning a lot about two friends through their never-ending text messages, voice mails, and emergency interruptions. I owe a big thanks to twenty-first-century media and technology for helping me better understand the exclusive and confidential rules of true friendship. If I didn't have a wireless connection, I'd be absolutely clueless on the subject.

Chapter 19

The sun peeks through the clouds, sending its warm rays over Palmville. It's early morning. My eyes are half open, but Frederick insists I let him outside. He leads the way down the stairs through the hall into the kitchen out the back screen door through the tall grass in the backyard and up one of our eternally ripe lemon trees. While Frederick peers through a grouping of lemons that hang from the tree, I lean back on the carved wooden bench, tucking a brightly printed canvas pillow under my head. Something startles Frederick. He shimmies down the tree, then gallops over to warn me. I look up to see a swarm of golden butterflies skywriting a message to me. It says, "Imagine if . . ." I can't make out the rest of the message because the butterflies decide to fly in all directions, creating a golden yellow cloud that floats far away. DREAM ENDS.

I hop out of bed with a burst of morning energy. This was the first dream I've had about Patch since Indigo and I decided to go on a search for him together. I race downstairs to report to the Dream-Checker-in-residence. She'll want to hear about the awesome details in living dream colors.

7:13 A.M.,
AVATAR KITCHEN

Indigo is in high spirits this morning. The breakfast menu, which is never quite the same, features pomegranate muffins with lemon-lime butter. I sample one, biting off just the crispy browned edge. "I had a dream last night!"

She spins around, her long Indian skirt following her dramatic move. "How wonderful. Tell me everything!"

"The golden butterflies were back. This time with a

message they wrote in the sky just for me. I know what they were saying too, even though they didn't actually finish the sentence."

Indigo isn't a fortune-teller, but she can predict what I'm about to say next. "Dad is on his way home!"

Indigo, who is now back behind the kitchen counter prepping my lunch for school, turns to me. Her voice cracks. "Really?" I pretend not to notice that her light morning mood is slowly darkening. She tries to keep up a cheerful tone. "Your lunch is ready, and I've got to get you to school now."

"Thanks, Mom." I grab my overstuffed book bag with my lunch crammed inside, feel for the postcard from Patch in my back pocket, and before I close the front door behind me, I shout to Frederick, "I'll see you later! Be a good cat. And I promise we'll have lots of playtime in the very near future."

7:58 A.M.,
PALMVILLE STREET

Indigo drives insanely slow today. She has no idea that the other drivers are tossing nasty sneers her way. She moves at her own pace, trying hard to protect me from the *dangerous* roads of our small-town paradise.

I look out the window while I casually mention, "Vera told me that the circumstances surrounding Patch were about timing."

Indigo, the super safe driver of all time, swerves the car, then realigns the vehicle and her mind. "She told you?"

For a more dramatic touch, I nod and don't say anything.

Indigo stutters as the car pulls to a stop in front of school. "You know it was a twist of fate how Patch and I met in the first place."

Pretending to know exactly what she means, I say, "I know."

Her shoulders sink back, and she's more relaxed now. "Vera just happened to be the one who introduced us."

I leap up off my seat. "What?"

"Vera told you how she introduced me to Patch the first day he got into town, right?"

I open the door and step out, then lean into the car. "Vera told me that she knew Patch, not that she introduced him to you. This changes everything!" I close the door and walk down the stairs in the direction of the school's main entrance.

Indigo just sits there in the car, staring at me. I calmly continue walking.

> **IMPORTANT FACT:** This new development stirs up a mountain-high pile of burning questions. It also sets off an uncomfortable feeling in my stomach that reminds me of the few times in my life when I have mixed pepperoni pizza with chocolate caramel swirl ice cream.

Chapter 20

I carefully place my essay number two at the center of Mr. Scuzzy's desk just as he walks into the classroom. He thanks me for giving more thought to the subject of twenty-first-century media and says that he looks forward to reading it. He adds, "I found your piece on second chances illuminating." Handing me the ripped paper with essay number one on it, he winks. "Next time, one page will be just fine."

"Sorry about that. Thanks, Mr. S."

OBERSERVATION: Maybe Misty didn't get me into trouble after all. Maybe because of her lack of note-passing skills, she actually provided me with an opportunity to show Mr. Scuzzy a side of myself that he wouldn't have seen if I hadn't been assigned the punishment essay in the first place.

FACT: Sometimes opportunities can arrive in mysterious ways.

12:13 P.M., CAFETERIA, PALMVILLE MIDDLE SCHOOL

Misty sips a pint-size container of milk while tapping her foot to an imaginary pop tune. When she sees me, she enthusiastically leaps up, spilling her drink over her mocha capris and polar bear hoodie. Wiping up the milk with a cafeteria napkin, Misty exclaims, "There's big news. Maxwell likes pomegranates! Just before I went to bed, I looked at the almost full moon and had the thought that Maxwell might like cake.

171

And he did! Your mom's special pomegranate cake has changed everything!"

I take out my PDA, pretending that I'm jotting down notes about Maxwell, but really I'm trying to determine the progress of my "real" case featuring Misty.

As I do this, Misty hands me a new piece of valuable evidence. "I can't remember the last time my mother baked anything for me. I would be shocked if she ever did anything special for me."

Tipping my hat to the side just over my eye, I offer, "The way you do for your animal friends."

Misty bursts out, "I just realized something monumental. I haven't rescued an animal or insect, not even a centipede, in forty-eight hours. It's all because of you!"

I input this flood of new data, careful not to raise suspicion about the true identity of the case's subject.

QUESTIONS: I wonder if the reason Misty hasn't rescued an animal in two days is because she's "getting a life." Maybe it's because she's making a new friend—me!

VERY IMPORTANT NOTE: Perhaps Misty spends all her free time surrounded by animals and insects because they're the only ones in her immediate family circle who appreciate her. It occurs to me that Misty shares the same trait as all of her animal friends. She is a highly appreciative friend.

FRIENDSHIP RULE #5: True friends appreciate each other on a daily basis.

Right on cue, Amy C. interrupts our lunch with a red-carpet entrance. She sits down next to me. "Portia, you look stressed. You don't have a snakebite, do you?" She looks over at Misty. "What are you girls talking about? Anything to share?"

I tell her as delicately as I can, "It's about the case, and it's confidential."

Sitting up as straight as a ruler, Amy narrows her eyes so her top and bottom eyelashes meet. "We've been friends forever, P. Avatar. And suddenly you stop spending time with me . . . and now you won't even have a simple conversation with me! I've just about had it. You

 173

clearly don't understand the true and beautiful meaning of friendship."

Misty steps in. "Portia is everything about friendship. She's kind, considerate, caring, and fun, too!"

Then it's my turn. "There's always room for a new friend in your life. That's true for everyone, including you, Amy."

Amy smiles with an extra large plastic grin. "Thanks for reminding me about that mucho important facto. W.H. and I are meeting again for, I don't know, the thirty-fifth time this week." Checking her heart-shaped watch, she says with a heavy Italian accent, "Ciao!" She stands up to leave the table, when Webster appears, carrying a heavy math textbook.

He hands the book to Amy. "Miss Clamdigger, you left this at our tutoring session yesterday."

Amy responds with the agility of a NASCAR driver and the smile of a celebrity starlet, "You mean our rendezvous!"

I step in and ask Amy, "Is that why you were with Webster? Why didn't you just tell me? Why the big mystery? You can tell me the truth. We're friends."

Amy stares at Misty when she asks me, "Are we?"

I respond, "Amy, just because Misty is a new friend

doesn't mean you're not my old friend anymore!"

She says with certainty, "There's a reason why people say three's a crowd."

"According to my mathematical calculations, one plus one plus one equals a potentially amazing combination."

Amy questions my logic. "Is that really possible?"

Before I can answer, Misty chimes in, "I think it's a great idea."

Then I add, "Would you think about it, please?"

Amy looks Misty up and down. "But New Girl and I are total opposites. Look at her. I would never wear brown anything!"

I insist, "We're all different. That's what's so cool."

FRIENDSHIP RULE #6: Every friend is one of a kind, just like an ocean stone or a butterfly wing.

Webster is getting noticeably antsy from all this girl talk. "I'll, uh, be getting back to my split pea soup."

Neither Amy, nor Misty, nor I take notice. We all just look at one another without speaking for the remaining ten seconds of lunch until the bell rings.

Chapter 21

I'm flying down the hill, fanning myself with my math quiz, which has the triangular-shaped letter A sketched across the front page and a personal note from Miss K. herself! It reads:

Portia, I enjoyed the answer to your bonus question immensely. You can imagine now why I entered the field of mathematics. I look forward to watching you develop your math skills at Palmville Middle School. I have great expectations for you!

As the perfect accent to my sunshiny and flowery mood, the air smells fresh without a hint of wildfires. It's been weeks since the Palmville skies were this blue. Change is in the air . . . and everywhere. I feel a sudden surge of energy from the math quiz victory, and from having also talked things out with Amy.

IMPORTANT NOTE: Since Amy and I have shared our thoughts, I have come to the conclusion that our friendship won't be exactly the same as it was before Misty entered the scene, but we'll still be friends.

FACT: It's a total mystery to me what will happen next.

3:38 P.M.,
CONTENTMENT (THE TENT)

Through the beaded entrance, I see Hap cleaning the grill, preparing for the approaching dinner crowd. He spots me and asks if I would please pick a couple of avocados for a salad he's creating. I step back outside, choosing the ripest fruit I can find.

Back inside The Tent, I hand Hap the avocados, which he gratefully accepts with a bow. "Much thanks, milady."

I play along and curtsy. "No problem." Then, switching the subject, I ask, "Have you seen Indigo?"

Hap's face tenses up.

I answer for him. "She's with Rock?"

Buddhist monks decide to chant in unison over the speakers as Hap nods slowly. "They left together about an hour ago."

I really wanted to talk more with Indigo about Vera's big deception and pursue my line of questioning about what both of them know (but aren't telling me) about Patch. I decide to see if Hap has any clues until Indigo returns to The Tent. "Would you mind if I asked you something?"

"As long as you don't mind if I cook while you talk."

"I'm totally used to that. No problem."

"I don't know where to begin."

"Just tell me what's on your mind."

"Hap, what's your opinion of friendship?"

He peels an avocado with grace and skill. "I'm all for it!"

"I was wondering, why would a friend tell you only half the truth?"

Pouring out tomatoes from a wooden bowl onto another cutting board, Hap thinks hard about my question, then offers me a tomato slice. "Are you talking about a good friend?"

"I thought so."

Sampling a bright red beet, he continues, "If she is a true friend, then she's probably got a good reason for being so secretive."

Then my PDA flashes red. It's Misty with an emergency text message.

To: pavatar@palmville.net
From: animalsrule@palmville.net

It's Maxwell! He won't stop eating the
pomegranate cake, and it's almost gone.
Come quick! There are only a few crumbs left.

Please bring cake! I repeat, please bring cake!

"Hap, Maxwell needs Indigo's pomegranate cake right away. He's starving!"

"Is Maxwell the friend you were telling me about?"

"I cannot disclose anything. It's for a case. And it's strictly confidential."

Without hesitation, he says, "Got it. But we've been out of the pomegranate cake since this morning. And it sounds like you need it right away."

With my detective sombrero firmly atop my head, I exclaim, "Cookies! Do you think we could make cookies instead?"

Hap already has the mixing bowl and industrial mixer revving up. "A spark of sheer brilliance." Starry-eyed, he adds, "You remind me of someone we both know very well."

Hap supervises as I mix, blend, create, and bake three batches of cookies. I decide to call them Pomegranate Perfections. As soon as they're out of the oven, I place them in a recycled tin and rush out of The Tent, straight to Misty's house for the rescue.

Halfway down the street, I turn and see Hap waving

to me outside The Tent's entrance. "You absolutely understand friendship. A friend in need . . . and so on!!"

"Thanks! You are one of the coolest older people I know!"

Hap laughs. "I'll take that as a compliment."

Then I turn back toward my destination for another rescue mission.

SPECIAL NOTE: Since Indigo will never open her eyes to Hap's obvious true love for her (besides, her heart is reserved for Patch), I hope that someday Hap finds the pure and perfect love he longs for 24/7.

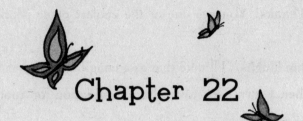

Chapter 22

5:18 P.M.,
MISTY'S BACKYARD

When I deliver the Pomegranate Perfections to Misty, she grabs the tin and runs off to attend to Maxwell. She promises to check in with any developments. My work is done for now, so I reverse my steps and find my way back home.

My focus will now be on following the latest lead in the Patch case. I am determined to track down Indigo and get her undivided attention without any more interruptions or excuses!

I slip into the kitchen through the back door. Indigo stands over our retro stove with a large wooden spoon in her hand. She turns to me and casually says, "I'm taking your advice to heart. I promise this time there'll be no tang to the linguini. Dinner will be early tonight, okay?"

"Okay."

She adds with a raised eyebrow, "I know about the Pomegranate Perfections."

"Hap told you?"

Indigo reassures me, "Don't worry, he didn't reveal any more details than that." She adjusts her single braid. "I tried one, and I think they're perfect! Would you consider letting me feature them on The Tent's new menu? They're just what I've been looking for."

A hundred-watt lightbulb goes on in my head. "Of course, Mom. Under one condition."

Indigo leans back slightly and takes a deep breath. "What would that be, Portia?"

Now it's me who takes a deep breath. "Please tell me the unabridged story of how Vera introduced you to Patch." Building momentum, I continue, "And what it was like when you first set eyes on him."

Indigo calmly squeezes a fresh lemon into two glasses of iced organic green tea. She hands me one of the glasses, and to my surprise, she begins the story of how Patch came into her life, as if the twelve years of waiting and wondering when I will meet my one and only father was never a subject of conversation at breakfast, lunch, or dinner.

As Indigo recounts "the story," my ears suddenly go deaf. Then slowly I hear the words floating into space, twirling toward me. Indigo tells me, "Patch was visiting from northern California. We were both so young. I don't remember very much."

I can't resist. "He wore a hat! I just know it!"

Indigo smiles with faraway eyes. "It was a cowboy hat."

"Are you sure that's what he wore? Memory can play all sorts of tricks on you. Was it really a cowboy hat?"

Indigo laughs as she continues to paint me a portrait. "It was made of straw and there were dried flowers woven around the rim."

"Patch wore flowers in his hair?" I wonder just how many details I can digest as I form a mental picture of him in my mind.

Indigo asks me, "What else can I tell you about him?"

I let out a big exhale. "How about everything!" A knock on our front door interrupts our delicate conversation. I know exactly who is standing on the other side of the door. "Why does Rock always have to get in the way of our lives? He's ruining this major life-will-never-be-the-same family breakthrough moment! I can't take him anymore!" I storm upstairs to my room.

A FEW MINUTES LATER,
MY BEDROOM

There's a light tap on my door. I shout, "I'm not hungry!"

Then I hear, "It's Misty."

In absolute disbelief, I call out, "Did you say 'Misty'?"

"Portia, open the door!"

I hesitate at first, then walk over to the door and open it. There she is, Misty Longfellow, in my house, outside my room, standing there with all her creatures, too! Frederick races through her legs, jumping onto my bed, anxious to get a front-row seat. "Does your mom know you're here?"

"Of course not. I ran away from home. I wouldn't share something like that with her. Besides, she's too busy to listen to me anyway." Misty steps inside my room and looks around like she's Dorothy just after she landed in Munchkinland. "It's positively perfect!"

Looking at Misty's pendant, her retainer case, and the old shoebox containing Maxwell, I ask, "You brought all your friends, too?"

Smiling, she says, "Of course! I can't think of a cooler place to run away to than the Avatar household."

Frederick sits on my bed, studying Misty's traveling circus. Maxwell is wrapped in the torn and worn fleece

 186

blanket that had previously served as his tent. Misty carefully takes him out of the shoebox and places him at the center of my throw rug. Frederick follows Maxwell's every move.

Indigo arrives with hot carob drinks topped with whipped soy cream for me and Misty and a bowl of mineral-enriched water for Maxwell. Carefully she slides the bowl next to Maxwell, who suddenly howls like an Alaskan wolf. Indigo quickly jumps into emergency mode, calmly handing out instructions to me and Misty. Within minutes, Maxwell is resting comfortably on one of my pillows in the far corner of my room (where Frederick has been sleeping), surrounded by bathroom towels.

Frederick cautiously approaches Maxwell, who hisses at anyone who tries to get close to him. Misty, Indigo, and I keep watch over Maxwell to determine exactly what's wrong, while Misty pleads, "It's my biggest wish in life that you'll let me and my animal friends live with you in your amazing home. I'm a highly cooperative person and I'm good with animals." Frederick brushes up against her right leg affectionately on cue.

Then something happens. Maxwell's growling stops,

and the room is suddenly silent. I look over at him. He appears to be in a trance now. He starts panting like he's just run a marathon. Then he sticks out his tongue at us. A collection of high-pitched squeals fills the room. Indigo rushes over to him. With her hands in the air, she says urgently, "I've got to go to The Tent to pick up goat's milk and alfalfa. I'll be back in ten minutes!"

Misty gently strokes Maxwell, while Frederick and I watch in awe as we see eight baby bunnies squirm around Maxwell's belly.

I whisper to Misty, "I think we should rename Maxwell Maxine!"

Chapter 23

Mrs. Longfellow samples a freshly baked Pomegranate Perfection. She and Indigo are finishing up a "long talk" about Misty's animal rescuing "situation." When Misty and I walk into the room, Mrs. Longfellow reaches out to hold Misty's hand. Misty freezes in her tracks.

OBSERVATION: Maybe Misty doesn't know how to react to her mother's hand-holding gesture because she's not used to it. It's possible that Misty might be entering a new, unknown universe that she doesn't understand yet, so she doesn't know what to do with herself.

IMPORTANT NOTE: Just like the Avatars, I wonder if the Longfellows are on their way to experiencing a major life-will-never-be-the-same family breakthrough.

9:23 P.M.,

AVATAR KITCHEN

The mockingbird sings his loud nightly tune outside our open kitchen window while Misty gathers Sweet Sunshine and Ralphie, checking three times that they're in their respective portable mini-homes. She also collects her knapsack and her overnight bag. One conspicuous piece of Misty's belongings is missing, though. It's Maxine, who's upstairs under Frederick's watchful eye, resting comfortably. Indigo and Mrs. Longfellow both agree that the happy mother and her octuplets should stay at the Avatars' for a while, at least until the bunnies are old enough to travel.

Misty gives me a big hug before stepping into her mom's just-washed car. "I am so proud to call you my friend, Portia Avatar."

From her opened backseat window, she calls, "Would you please give Maxine and the babies a kiss good night for me?" I stand at the edge of my pebbly driveway watching Misty, her mother, and her mother's shiny car disappear into the distance.

CASE FINDINGS: Perhaps the reason Misty has been so stray-animal-obsessed is because she saw herself as a stray. With busy parents and a brother sent off to an out-of-state boarding school, she felt ignored and alone on a twenty-four-hour basis.

CONCLUSION: Maybe now that Misty has a little more practice in making friends, she might start seeing herself differently. Maybe she won't hide behind orphaned bunnies, spiders, and three-legged crickets so much anymore. Maybe she will hang out with more human types (like me!).

The Case of Misty Longfellow: The Mystifying Animal Rescuer is now officially closed.

Before I step inside, I take off my hat and tuck it in my side pocket. I feel for my postcard, which is still there. I take it out and study it.

Then I look up at the stars and think how badly I want to share my case findings with my extraordinary detective father. I start to count the sparkly miracles in the sky one by one. When I get to twelve, I look down and there's Frederick. He stretches his whole body up toward me until I'm forced to pick him up. I cradle him like a baby, rocking him back and forth. "Aren't the bunnies amazing, Freddy Fred Frederick?"

He licks my hand as if to tell me, "Thank you for bringing me all these new little friends. I know that they're going to fill up my life, like the way the stars are filling up the sky right now with their bright light and deep mystery."

Frederick's purring competes with the lone mockingbird's song. I just stare at the universe above us and wonder what my family would look like if Patch were home with us right now. Would the sounds I'm hearing be different? If I stood in front of the mirror, would I recognize myself?

Chapter 24

Frederick takes a break from baby-bunny watch. He jumps onto my bed while I prepare for the big Patch Powwow tonight. He swipes at my hand as I create the itinerary for our discussion on my loyal PDA. Now that the Misty case is closed, I can focus exclusively on the case of my missing father.

NOTES FOR THE PATCH POWWOW TONIGHT:

1. Figure out what Vera knows about Patch.

2. Learn more about the postcard and the mysterious correspondence between Patch and Vera.

3. Create a new plan for the search.

4. Find Patch!

I try to think about how to use this precious powwow time when I hear a familiar laugh downstairs. I cannot believe Rock is here again! I dial our phone number.

Indigo picks up after one ring. Surprised, she asks, "Portia, where are you?"

"I'm upstairs. Is he here again?"

"You mean Rock?"

"Shh! I don't want him to know that we're talking about him."

"He stopped by to give us the wonderful news that the fires are finally under control. Isn't that beautiful?"

"Yes, it's great. Now please, Mom. He has to go now. We're having our powwow tonight, and he's not invited."

"Of course. Hold on one minute." She hands the phone to Rock. I cannot believe this!

QUESTION: Where do mothers get their amazing talent for bad timing?

Rock asks in a cheerful way, "Is this Portia Avatar, girl detective and math whiz?"

"Affirmative."

Rock chuckles. "I'll just take a minute of your time. I know you've got an important meeting scheduled soon."

"That's right."

"Here's my proposal. We've got a dog at the station. His name is Mack."

Pretending to care, I answer, "Uh-huh."

"We're all dog people at the station, but what we really need is a civilizing influence. It can get pretty darn rowdy with just us guys." He laughs out loud at what he's just said.

Still pretending to care, I mumble, "Uh-huh."

"I'd like to adopt Miss Maxine as an honorary member of the Palmville Hook and Ladder Company No. 1. I understand Misty's mother won't allow any more pets, so I want to step in and make an offer. Once Miss Maxine is

 195

finished weaning her bunnies, it would be my honor, and I speak for the rest of the guys too, to take her back to the station and give her a home there." I'm stunned at first. This is not what I was expecting from the "I'm so heroic, look at my muscles" firefighter. Rock is thrown off by my silence. "Portia, are you still there?"

"That sounds awesome." Then I gently hang up. After a handful of giggles from downstairs, I hear the front door finally close. I rush to the window and see Rock heading toward his red pickup truck. I find myself waving to him and shouting out my open window, "Thanks, Rock!" As soon as his truck zooms away out of view, I leave Maxine and her bunnies to check in with Indigo downstairs. Frederick is at my heels.

All I can think about now is what I will learn tonight about my mysterious family past.

6:44 P.M.,

AVATAR KITCHEN

I set the table for three. The phone rings. It's Misty, checking on the bunnies. Indigo hands me the phone but signals with her insistent brown eyes for me to make it short.

I lean back on the living room couch pillow and give Misty a full report on Maxine. She laughs when I tell her how Frederick is Maxine's new best friend, and how he keeps watch over the bunnies almost every minute of the day. And she's amazed that Rock and his firefighter buddies are going to adopt Maxine. She's already planning weekly visits to the station. Then my phone call is interrupted by an incoming message from Amy. I ask Misty to hold on while I pick it up. Cautiously I say, "Hi, Amy."

Sensing a complete attitude makeover, Amy speaks softly and slowly. "I'm checking in on you and your new oh-so-secret case."

"It's officially closed as of today."

"That's too bad. I've got the final sketches for your fabulous new look. I guess you won't be needing them anymore. I even have some samples."

"I'd love to see what you've got! You never know when I'll stumble on a new case."

Amy tests the water. "Does that mean you won't be spending as much time with Misty?"

I respond, "Actually, now that the bunnies are here, I'll be seeing a lot of Misty."

"Bunnies?"

"It's a long story."

Amy's voice brightens when she says, "I've always wanted a bunny!"

"Really? Maybe you should come by and see them."

"I'd love to. That is, if I'm welcome."

I can tell that Amy is still feeling left out of the newly forming friendship triangle, even though I tried to explain to her that three is definitely not a crowd. So I suggest, "Let's all meet up after school tomorrow."

Amy agrees and also informs me, "I've developed a few ideas to spice up Misty's look too. I think she's going to like what I've come up with."

"Perfection . . . Misty! She's on the other line. I've got to get back to her."

"Wait, Portia."

"Yes, Amy?"

"I'm sorry."

I smile to myself. I've never heard Amy say these words to me before in the history of our friendship. Then

I apologize. "I'm sorry too. I never meant to make you feel left out. You're so totally my BFF!"

OBSERVATION: Just like families, friendships are tested too, and those tests can lead to breakthroughs and new beginnings.

QUESTION: Is this a new beginning of my friendship with Amy that includes our new friend, Misty?

FRIENDSHIP RULE #7: Just like all the stars and all the planets in our ever-expanding universe, friendships are constantly changing too.

I hang up with Amy and quickly switch back to Misty. "Misty? Are you still there? Do you read me?"

"I'm here!"

"Sorry about that. Now I've got to go to an important meeting for another case, the one about Patch. Before I hang up, there's big news to report."

"Yes?"

"I found a new home for one of Maxine's little bunnies."

"Who? Where?"

"Amy C. wants one."

Misty's mood shifts. Suddenly she's quiet. "Oh."

"It turns out she has new fashion concepts that she designed just for you. She wants you to see them tomorrow."

Misty is truly mystified. "For me? I'm beyond amazed!"

"Oh, and I found another home for one of the baby bunnies too."

"Awesome. I hope it's not too far away."

"It's right here! Indigo is letting me keep one. Frederick has taken a real liking to the striped one. We're going to call him Tiger."

"Fantastic! Oh no, I've got to go. My mom is actually making dinner for me and my dad tonight. It's a major miracle. Thank you and Frederick and Indigo for looking after Maxine and her little ones."

"They're fitting right in to the family circle. See you tomorrow!"

Just as I hang up, my PDA lights up again. I'm convinced it's Misty, with a burning follow-up question about Maxine that can't wait until the morning, but I'm mistaken. It's Webster!

Bravely, I take the call. "Hello?"

"This is Webster. Webster Holiday. Did I wake you up?"

"Of course not. It's dinnertime!"

"Right. I knew that. About that question I was going to ask you."

"Yes?"

"What are you having for dinner?"

My face crumples up like an old paper bag. "What?"

Stammering slightly, Webster continues, "Dinner. An evening meal usually consisting of several courses."

All I can think of is, "Pomegranate cookies."

"I see. Portia, I'd like to share something with you. It's about pomegranates."

With great anticipation, I hang in there. "Oh?"

"The pomegranate is one of the earliest cultivated fruits. It has been traced back as far as 3000 B.C."

I'm not exactly sure how to respond to this historical footnote. "I've really got to go now. We're having a special guest tonight."

Insistent, Webster keeps talking. "About my question." There's total silence on my end of the phone. Then

I hear, "What would be the probability of me walking you to school tomorrow morning?"

In a hurry to end this embarrassing conversation, I say, "Approximately one hundred percent." And just like that, I hang up.

> **IMPORTANT FACTS:** Webster Holiday has just asked Portia Avatar on her first almost date! He's walking me to school tomorrow, and all my clothes are dirty!

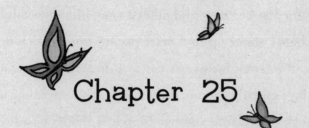

Chapter 25

Vera and Indigo each lean on Indian silk pillows on opposite sides of our living room couch. I sit on the floor across from them reading and rereading the postcard from Patch. On the dark wooden coffee table between us are a few leftover Pomegranate Perfections and two clay mugs containing steaming hot herbal tea. With my free hand, I hold a small cup of hot carob milk and take a sip. We've made some progress in our discussion so far, but still nothing groundbreaking has resulted from our powwow. I can't stand the delicate dance around the subject any longer, so I decide to shake up the party with a question. "Vera, where is he?"

Vera lifts her mug and takes a sip. "I don't know."

Then I stand up and start pacing up and down the room. Frederick meows at me as I do this, then remembers he's on baby-bunny duty and quickly races upstairs to check on Maxine and her brood. "I thought you were here to help. Once upon a time, you were my friend."

Indigo chimes in, "Patch could be anywhere, Portia."

Then Vera dramatically places her mug down on the table and stands up. She starts pacing alongside me. "Portia is right. I can help. I know where Patch is!" I stop, frozen on the hardwood floor. She continues, "He's here with us right now."

I'm not fooled for a minute. "Is this just another trick to avoid the subject?"

Indigo sits at the edge of the couch with a puzzled look on her face. Vera looks at Indigo and says, "Let's turn our attention away from trying to find a location for Patch. What if we create a shared memory of Patch for Portia instead? Maybe together we can offer her an image of him to help with her search."

To my astonishment, Indigo agrees.

We settle back to our original positions in the room and soon the most romantic story of two young people falling in love for the first time comes to life before my eyes and ears.

I hold my breath as Vera begins, "Patch was a visitor from out of town on his way down the coast to help build a home for a family in need. He was gentle and charming and made me laugh."

I can't contain myself. "What color hair did he have?"

I wish I had a pair of supersonic glasses so I could see what Vera sees when she describes Patch. "It was brown, but he had blue eyes. I remember how bright they were and how they sparkled when he spoke."

I put my hand over my heart to slow down its race-car speed. "What was he doing at your store?"

Smiling, Vera tells me, "He was collecting things for the house he was about to build."

"Where?"

"I never found out the name of the town. Anyway, he moved on from there after a few months. That's when we lost touch. He wrote that postcard just after he left California."

I gently slide my hand over the front of the postcard and take a closer look at it.

Indigo takes a turn. "I was stopping by Vera's the day Patch first got here. I wanted advice on a new product line we were selling at the store. That's when I was working at Naturally Natural."

Vera laughs. She looks over at Indigo. "Remember that truck?"

Indigo playfully rolls her eyes.

I continue with my line of questioning. I turn to Indigo. "What happened when you looked into each other's eyes?"

To answer this question, Indigo closes her eyes. "The first thing I noticed about him was that he was tan, which immediately told me he liked the outdoors."

I find myself catching my breath, the way I would after a bike ride up a steep hill or after spending a long day at the beach. "He was tall, right?"

"Yes, he was tall!"

I feel warm, salty tears travel down my cheeks. "Why didn't you tell me that before?"

Vera quietly observes us when Indigo confesses, "This has been a painful process for me, too. I see how hard you work to find him, and I don't have anything to offer you."

I stand up and sit next to Indigo on the couch, wrapping my arms around her.

"This is perfect!"

Indigo tears up. "I wish he could see how beautiful you are, Portia. When I close my eyes and picture Patch, I see a lot of you in him, especially your curious nature and determined spirit!"

I feel my heartbeat again with my hand and leave it there until it slows down to a normal pace. Patch is a part of me. He feels real to me, even though I can't see him.

Vera quietly excuses herself. "We made some real progress here tonight. I'll see you next week, that is, if I'm invited. I'd like to come on board to help with the search." She reaches her hand out for mine.

I hold Vera's hand and lead her to the door, with Indigo right next to me. "Three is my new favorite number!"

Tonight I heard the first chapter of the story of my missing father. I wonder how far a memory can travel, and how long it can last. If Indigo and Vera can recall details of what they remember about Patch more than twelve years ago, can other memories from that time be conjured up across the globe in Patch's mind too? Does my father think about Indigo or Palmville or Vera while he's riding on a fast-moving train across a rural countryside, when he's sitting on a white sandy beach squinting at the sun, when he's washing his hair in the cold blue sea, or when he drifts to sleep under a dark and endless starry sky? What ever happened to that rusty old truck?

I close my eyes and make a plan to dream about Patch tonight, to take the beginning of the story I just heard and imagine the ending.

FACT: Now with Vera on the team to find Patch, and a Patch Powwow every Sunday night, we'll definitely be moving closer to finding him.

VERY IMPORTANT NOTE: Maybe the reason Vera hadn't told me about Patch and his first meeting with Indigo before now was because she wanted me to hear it at just the right moment in just the right place, like tonight at home with Indigo there too.

FRIENDSHIP RULE #8: True friends surprise you in miraculous ways.

DORK
diaries

Tales from a
NOT-SO-
Fabulous Life

She's a self-proclaimed dork. She
has the coolest pen ever. She keeps
a top-secret diary.
Read it if you dare.

By Rachel Renee Russell

From Aladdin
Published by Simon & Schuster

FREE Club for you and your BFFs on BeaconStreetGirls.com!

If you loved this book, you'll love hanging out with the **Beacon Street Girls** (BSG)! **Join the BSG** (and their dog Marty) for virtual sleepovers, fashion tips, celeb interviews, games and more!

And with **Marty's secret code** (below), start getting **totally free stuff right away!**

To get **$5** in **MARTY $ MONEY** (one per person) go to **www.BeaconStreetGirls.com/redeem** and follow the instructions, while supplies last.

Real life. Real you.

Total Knockout

Don't miss
any of these
terrific
Aladdin Mix
books.

Chasing Blue

Portia's Exclusive and
Confidential Rules
on True Friendship

The Secret Identity
of Devon Delaney

Hershey Herself

Four Truths and a Lie

Do you love the color pink?
All things sparkly? Mani/pedis?

These books are for you!

From Aladdin
Published by Simon & Schuster

FIVE GIRLS. ONE ACADEMY. AND SOME SERIOUS ATTITUDE.

CANTERWOOD CREST

by Jessica Burkhart

TAKE THE REINS

CHASING BLUE

BEHIND THE BIT

TRIPLE FAULT

Don't forget to check out the website for downloadables, quizzes, author vlogs, and more!
www.canterwoodcrest.com

FROM ALADDIN M!X   PUBLISHED BY SIMON & SCHUSTER